APPLE
TO THE CORE

By Marc Lovell

APPLE TO THE CORE
APPLE SPY IN THE SKY
SPY ON THE RUN
THE SPY WITH HIS HEAD IN THE CLOUDS
THE SPY GAME
HAND OVER MIND
A VOICE FROM THE LIVING
THE SECOND VANETTI AFFAIR
THE BLIND HYPNOTIST
DREAMERS IN A HAUNTED HOUSE
AN ENQUIRY INTO THE EXISTENCE OF VAMPIRES
A PRESENCE IN THE HOUSE
THE IMITATION THIEVES
THE GHOST OF MEGAN

APPLE TO THE CORE

MARC LOVELL

PUBLISHED FOR THE CRIME CLUB BY
DOUBLEDAY & COMPANY, INC.
GARDEN CITY, NEW YORK
1983

All of the characters in this book
are fictitious, and any resemblance
to actual persons, living or dead,
is purely coincidental.

Library of Congress Cataloging in Publication Data

Lovell, Marc.
Apple to the core.

I. Title.
PR6062.O853A84 1983 823'.914
ISBN 0-385-18749-1
Library of Congress Catalog Card Number 82-48708

First Edition

APPLE
TO THE CORE

CHAPTER 1

Apple felt his way along the wall. His touch was not the blind's delicate tickling with fingertips, but the heavy-handed scraping of someone rendered sightless by the dark. Visibility, however, had no bearing on the matter: more than enough early morning light was seeping into the hall-way. Apple's firm contact with the wall was to give himself a feeling of security.

Danger lay ahead, it lay behind, and it lay on either side. The silence in the building seemed more to threaten than assure. It hinted at the enemy patiently waiting.

Appleton Porter went on at the same quiet, cautious pace. He took his hand off the wall while passing the door of apartment 3B, through which, faintly, came a BBC voice. It was reading the seven A.M. news.

Hearing that the Queen had a cold and so would not be attending the initial events of the London Music Week, due to start tomorrow, Apple passed on. He returned to his touchstone of security in matching time with the return of silence.

Appleton Porter was wearing a track suit, blue with a red stripe down sleeves and legs. His white sneakers were grey with age. In his hip pocket, itself added unorthodoxly to the track suit, was a hard object with the outlines of a chop.

Reaching a corner, where carpeted stairs went down, Apple stopped and looked back. The door of 3A was open.

Through the space came an atmosphere of tension. It was so potent that to Apple it seemed like a form of heat.

After licking the dryness from his lips, Apple moved onto the staircase. He went down in quiet caution, one hand rubbing the rail. The danger was growing.

Apple, aged twenty-eight, had a pale face with a scattering of freckles. These spots were the same sandy hue as his neat-cut hair and the eyebrows that sloped upward centrally in an angle of wonder, concern, doubt.

The face was averagely good-looking. This had never been accepted by its owner. He had always been purblinded by what he saw as drawbacks: the insipid colouring, the freckles, and that paleness which showed so brutally the blushes that were the second largest bane of his existence. Bane number one was his height.

Appleton Porter was six feet, seven inches tall. It had a bearing on everything in his life, from relationships to career, from clothing sizes to malignant doorways. After ten years of being nearly a foot taller than the standard Englishman, Apple still winced at the whimsical smiles of passers-by, cringed inside at the cruel shouts from children, while somehow ignoring that both these occurrences were rare.

Always Apple treated people who were taller than himself with such exaggerated consideration that they soon disliked him intensely. He forgave this, explaining it away privately as envy. Envy he knew about. Himself he gave it to undersized losers and stunted no-hopers.

Apple reached the hallway below. It was as deserted as the one he had just left. That gave no comfort. As he started down the next flight of stairs, his heart began tapping at more than its usual speed.

A board underfoot squeaked. Apple would have frozen and waited, except that time was of the essence. He went on down and turned onto the final staircase.

In his mind Apple pictured the open doorway above. Inside, in the dimness, the figure was standing taut, teeth showing, while listening acutely for the expected signal, the one that would mean it was safe to begin the escape.

Quickly, Apple dissolved the picture. He knew he might be tempted to let his imagination work on it and have the figure come out before the all-clear.

Tightening his nostrils at thoughts of the possible consequences, Apple hurried over the final steps and came into the entrance hall. His heart was tapping faster now.

The hall was spacious, with a table between stairs and front door. The table was used only for mail, a pile of which lay on the mat under the door's letter-slot. The sorting was left to whomever arrived first after deliveries.

With a twinge of guilt, Apple turned away. He went along a passage beside the staircase. He crouched in extra caution when going by a door on which was a plate stating ADMINISTRATION. Passing it safely, he strode on to the passage end.

Apple was unaware of his tongue bulging out his bottom lip as he gently, gently drew back a bolt, turned a handle, drew open the building's rear door. Leaving it wide, he went at tiptoe speed back along the passage.

In the hall, Apple leaned on the bannister rail, pointed his face upward, took a deep breath—and hissed. Then he stood aside. His attention and nervousness he divided between the stairs and the landlord's nearby door.

From above came a scuffling, a light drumming. It sounded like a spiky object being rolled around by someone taken by a mood of glee. The noise grew steadily in volume. Apple's heartbeat seemed to do the same.

At the head of the stairs Monico appeared. Eyes gleaming, tongue hanging out from his gaping mouth, he came hurtling down the final steps, ducked to go under the table, which he nevertheless scraped with his back, and coming out at the other end executed a neat turn by the door. He ran ahead of Apple along the passage.

The dog was an Ibizan Podenco, a breed peculiar to the Mediterranean island of Ibiza. It was odd in several other ways. While close to normal in habit and disposition, in appearance the type was liked mainly out of generosity.

Take a large greyhound, starve it until its knees knocked, lengthen the snout by a couple of inches, dye the whole animal a pale ginger, and finally stand it rear-end first into a gale so that the coat was roughened—that was an Ibizan Podenco.

In an untidy backyard, Apple drew the door quietly to its jamb. He grinned with relief. Patting the pork chop in his hip pocket, he went out to an alley and ran off in pursuit of Monico.

The Bloomsbury block of apartments called Harlequin Mansions had a no-pets rule. It was enforced with even greater passion than the stricture against offending the elegant Edwardian facade with laundry or other clues of habitation.

The landlord was a strange man, considering his calling. He liked children. He would give welcome to a couple with new-born twins and three toddlers, yet turn away the owner of any creature more active than a tortoise.

For years Apple had approved. But then he had acquired Monico, during a stay in Ibiza. Not wanting to leave the home where he had lived so long, he had decided to break the rule, even though still approving of it in theory. For days after that, he had slept badly.

While waiting for his dog to be released from the mandatory stay in quarantine kennels, as a guard against rabies entering the United Kingdom, Apple had worked out operational details. He would give the dog an outing every morning and evening. Weekends, Friday to Monday, using a borrowed or rented car, he would go to the country cottage which he had recently been willed by a relative, where Monico could have total freedom.

Everything was working as expected. A placid animal with an aversion to barking, Monico quickly adapted to the new life-style and accepted the training relating to escape. He was an ideal pet and an understanding companion. More, he had given Apple something which his daily life had formerly lacked—drama.

This, however, was seen by Apple as trauma. He didn't know how thoroughly he enjoyed the twice-daily risk or the rule-breaking guilt. He didn't even realize that he always seemed to step on the same squeaky board.

Apple was compensating. He was giving himself what he ought to have been getting from his career, and rarely did.

Appleton Porter worked for British Intelligence. He had done so since leaving university. But the times that he had been sent out into the field, as an agent on a mission, could be counted on the fingers of one thumbless hand.

There were drawbacks. Apple's chief, Angus Watkin, as well as other, more mysterious figures in the lofty levels of the service that were known as Upstairs, didn't like his height. It made the dimming of his presence a near impossibility. A good agent should be seen as one of the herd. That Apple could never do, short of convening a mob of seven-footers.

Next in the descending scale was the fact that Apple had a sympathetic nature. It was unlikely, his dossier stated under the heading of REMARKS, that he would be able to act with the ruthlessness that was often needed in espionage work.

Third, Apple was a blusher. A form of sympathy turned inward, it was a condition he had never been able to fully control, though he had tried many so-called cures over the years. Apple was forced to agree with REMARKS that a permanent cure was improbable.

The one he was currently using, bought, as usual, through a magazine advertisement, gave easement at the moment of the blush. But, like all the others, its effectiveness was sure to fade in time, due to familiarity.

REMARKS said finally that Appleton Porter was addicted to collecting odds and ends of information, none of which had the slightest value. The hoarding of trivia bespoke a want of emotional maturity.

After these four major strikes against Apple, it seemed irrelevant that he had not sparkled during his training period. At the country mansion called Damian House he had scored medium to poor in the vital arts: lying, acting, unarmed combat, resistance to physical pain, tolerance for alcohol, marksmanship. Only in two divisions had he scored a ten out of ten, and those scores he had already owned when he arrived. One was in security clearance, the other languages. The latter was the reason he had been enrolled in Intelligence in the first place.

Apple was a linguist. He spoke six foreign tongues with perfect fluency, another five with skill but an accent that was discernible to the knowing, and several more with a workmanlike competence.

He had taken up languages as a boy when a doctor told him that an accomplishment was the best way of losing the blushing habit. Apple had gained much, but lost nothing. He was never sure whether he should remember that doctor with warmth or coldness.

Warmth, that would have to be the answer if Apple were to take the matter as a serious question. His chosen field had given him a good, pleasant life. He was a senior official at the United Kingdom Philological Institute, where his undercover work was known about by nobody, and where he picked up a monthly paycheck to go with the one he got from Intelligence.

For that second wage Apple did work that was rewarding, though only in a cerebral sense. He double-checked decoded transcriptions in search of that one word that could change the whole gist; he wrote letters in whatever language was required; he listened to tapes of suspected agents' voices to judge on national origin; he sat in as translator on small meetings and large, high-level conferences. The work had everything but excitement. And romance. And intrigue.

Apple was an avid and poignant reader of spy fiction.

The morning outing went more or less as usual. Apple walked and jogged. He politely looked away when Monico visited a lamppost. While breakfasting on tea and a bacon sandwich in a workers' cafe, he didn't feel uncomfortable about his dog being outside, for Monico had his pork chop.

Many people looked with interest at the passing pair. These looks Apple interpreted with satisfaction as admiring. Another of the many factors which Apple had never recognized, at least not consciously, was that Monico bore a strong resemblance to himself.

By eight o'clock the pair were safely back in the flat. After showering, Apple put on his robe to stroll the spacious, high-ceilinged rooms and smoke his first cigarette of the day. The robe was in a large-check tartan of bellowing colours. Apple often wished he had the courage to be so sartorially outrageous in public.

The suit he put on presently was subdued to the point of being morose. At close range, a faint stripe could be discerned running across the dark material. This horizontal effect, Apple felt, tended to lessen his height, as did the tiny block design in his tie and socks. His shoes had the minimum of heel.

At twenty minutes past eight, giving Monico a pat that was friendly without being patronizing, Apple left the apartment. On his way downstairs he walked with a heavy step and whistled raucously.

In the entrance hall he met the landlord, who was sorting letters on the table, and who looked up with a dead smile. He said, "Good morning, Mr. Porter."

Apple gave back the greeting jovially, adding, "It's a beautiful spring day, Mr. Lampton. Not a breath of wind."

"Oh? You've been out already?"

Apple corrected with a fast, "Balcony. I stepped out onto my balcony for a minute."

The landlord blinked at him steadily. "I thought that window was jammed."

"I fixed it last night," Apple said. "Honestly."

"I see, Mr. Porter."

"So I stepped outside and held up a wet finger. You know. The way people do."

The landlord blinked on. Tall as far as the average was concerned, he had a craggy sixty-year-old face and black hair that looked like a wig. His green tweed suit was in its limp dotage, as droopy as slime.

Apple nodded convincingly. The landlord gave his attention back to the mail. "There's nothing for you, Mr. Porter," he said. "And I would have been happy to fix that window."

"Oh, I know, I know."

"I only heard of it through one of my other residents, to whom you'd mentioned it. You *can* come to me, you know, when you have problems in 3A. I don't mind."

"I'm sure of that, Mr. Lampton."

"I wouldn't bother you. I'd slip in during the day while you were out at work."

Showing his teeth like a politician, Apple explained as he edged towards the door that he enjoyed playing handyman, he really did, and that in any case nothing ever went wrong in the flat. It was perfect.

The landlord looked up again, showing an expression of mild astonishment. Apple escaped to the street.

Striding to keep in tune with his hurrying nerves, he told himself that Charles Lampton had not the slightest suspicion of rules being broken. He was simply being your standard landlord. He was no happier with a non-complaining resident than was an army officer when the ranks didn't grumble. There was certainly no need to panic; to consider bribery, moving or the fitting of new locks. No need at all.

Some minutes passed before Apple left the strife behind, which he did with a sigh. His nerves settled in a disgruntled way and he slowed to a normal walk.

Apple went along a street behind the British Museum. The morning being so fresh and pretty, he decided not to travel by underground train, but to bus over to Kensington, where the United Kingdom Philological Institute had its home.

Thinking of the weather returned Apple to his strife, to the slip he had made in remarking on the windless morning. It had been stupid and careless, he mused. It had been, in fact, the kind of innocuous-seeming thing that to an agent on a mission could mean the difference between life and death.

Apple was discomforted. Suddenly, to him came an awful question. It was one which usually mocked at him only on those rare nights when he suffered a bout of insomnia, due to the rash drinking of tea too close to bedtime.

Was it not sensible of Upstairs to so seldom make use of his services as an operative in the field?

Fortunately, there was no need of an answer. Apple was saved from that by a diversion.

The car was large and black. It drew swiftly into the

kerb a little ahead of where Apple was walking. It was that, the fast reduction of speed, that took his attention. He noted a male driver and one passenger in the back, also male.

As the car stopped—Apple almost level at that point—the rear nearside door opened. However, instead of the expected, the passenger hustling out on some errand of urgency, the man called, "Excuse me, sir."

There being no one else around, Apple strode to the car. He asked, "Can I help you?"

The man was leaning back into his place at the far end of the seat after having opened the door. Apple bent to keep him in view, though view was limited because of the man's hat. The driver was looking the other way.

"I wonder if you could give me directions to Seven Sisters Road, please," the passenger said.

Apple pointed. "It's straight on. You can't miss it."

"I'm sorry. Could you speak up, please. I'm a trifle hard of hearing."

Apple bent lower and leaned closer, so that his head was almost inside the body of the car. He began, "If you go straight on along—"

That was as far as he got. The rest was chopped off by the shove. It caught him in the small of the back. He jerked forward, his head snapping, and fell inside. He landed on his hands and knees on the limousine's carpeted floor. His left shoulder was beside the passenger's knees.

Apple felt only surprise, thinking he'd been hit accidentally by a hurrying passer-by, until the next shove came, which was immediately. It was the result of the door being slammed into its frame and against the soles of his shoes. Again he jerked forward. He hit the farther door with his head. It hurt.

The car moved away with a smooth swoop and the driver said, "See how easy that was?"

All fields of endeavour have their traditions. Mountaineering, philately, mining, kite-flying, theology, or whatever—each, from the sublime to the eccentric, has its own customs and forms, themselves ranging from absurdity to the profound. No actor would whistle in the dressing-room, no soldier would go into battle with dirty boots, no circus performer would dream of wishing a colleague good luck.

Open and widespread fields have few traditions, the obscure and limited have the most: politics is almost without, while book-collecting has enough to fill a first edition. Security for minorities can always be found in arcane possession.

Naturally, therefore, there are many traditions in the world of espionage. Some are as wise as not eating pork in an R-less month, most as petty and pointless as needlework to a lumberjack.

One of the former is that greetings should always be muted. Whether you met a fellow-agent by arrangement on Tower Bridge at midnight or by accident in the middle of the Sahara, whether you liked the man or not and even if you hadn't seen him for years, you kept the greeting subdued, casual, distant, and made do with a nod if you were a hardened professional.

Although this was taken as sophistication, it made sense, in accordance with laws relating to other situations. Never give anything away. Never presume that the other person is all that he seems. Never assume that you are unobserved or unheard. Never take for granted that any others who might be present have been given clearance. Never relax your vigilance. Never, ever underestimate the enemy.

In any case, as someone had once said in Apple's hearing, "There are very few friendships in the Service." Someone else had added the cold topper, "And none possible out of it."

So when Apple got up from the floor and sat at the opposite end of the seat from the passenger, whom he ignored completely, he didn't slap the driver's shoulder and say, "Hey, Bill, you old bastard." He folded his arms and near-yawned a, "Nice day."

Bill Burton, whose voice Apple had recognized when he'd asked, "See how easy that was?" glanced around from his expert driving. "A beautiful day. Makes you feel glad to be alive."

"Indeed it does."

"Can I drop you somewhere?"

"Kensington would do me nicely."

"Right you are."

The car went on. Bill Burton muttered curses at other drivers, the passenger hummed lightly while watching the scene through the window beside him.

Apple, feeling like a pro, was determined not to spoil things by asking what this was all about. He had a flicker of excitement. It was flicker and not flame because he reasoned that Bill Burton's rhetorical question about easiness had been for the passenger, not himself.

He, Apple, was being used in brief passing, the way a teacher might use a piece of chalk. It was common practice. Victims in trial runs had to be people who were unaware of the situation yet would require neither apology nor explanation.

Apple looked along the seat from the corners of his eyes. The passenger, plainly dressed, was in the early thirties. His face was so ordinary and forgettable that Apple knew him to be a full-time operative. He was one of the herd.

So yes, Apple thought, his flicker of excitement sinking

lower, this performance was for the pro's benefit and not a possible mission for Porter, Appleton.

Apple mused on the edge of glumness that if he had been a pro himself, instinct would have warned him that the direction-enquiry routine was danger. But then, these people were on his own side, so instinct didn't come into it. He was doing fine.

Cheering, Apple looked with affection at the driver. They had worked together once on a caper in Paris, when Bill Burton had been Apple's back-up man. It was a role he played often.

Burton was plump and fortyish. His features were passably and blandly good-looking. He would have been a herdman except for a prominent scar on one cheek. That memorable item put him in the middle of the game, between being a full-time operative and a member of the class known as the faceless ones, to which Apple belonged. These people were used rarely and more often than not because of a speciality: lip-reading, safe-breaking, or any of a hundred peculiar abilities.

While Bill Burton never took on a mission himself, he was frequently involved. He was an excellent driver, a crack shot with a pistol, and he had that scar—which had been caused by him falling on a broken bottle when he was an infant. It enabled him to be used as stage dressing if a scene called for someone to stand there and look dangerous.

Well, Apple thought, at least I'm here in an Upstairs car with a pair of first-class agents. And I'm playing it right, as cool as a cucumber.

He asked, "What's this all about?" His leg twitched. He did wish he wouldn't keep disappointing himself like this.

Bill Burton glanced aside. "Your guess is as good as mine, old son," he said. "You know as well as I do how our Angus's mind works."

"Yes, I do," Apple said. So it was an Angus Watkin caper. "Or rather, no, I haven't the foggiest idea."

"I know what you mean, and you know what I mean."

"Precisely."

"Our Angus has large eyes, big ears and a small mouth."

"He's not exactly gabby, true."

"So *I* can't tell you anything."

If that was an invitation, it either never arrived or wasn't going to be acknowledged. The passenger went on humming and gazing out of the window.

Apple decided nastily that he was bluffing; he didn't know a damn thing; he wasn't in *that* solid Upstairs. Angus Watkin wouldn't tell his own mother where he was born, unless he wanted something from her, which he would use against his father.

Bill Burton swung the limousine around Marble Arch through the stream of traffic. Neatly he cut in front of a cab, from which came an angry hoot. Burton grumbled, "They're a bloody menace, these taxies."

The passenger stopped humming. Looking around he asked, "Heard the latest?"

Apple said, "No." Burton said, "What?"

"It came from the top, close to heaven, and has a Very label, if not a Most."

"Which means," Bill Burton said, "that only seven hundred thousand people know about it, including the charwoman who cleans out the baskets."

"And her son who's got a ham-radio set."

"Plus his girl-friend who has it off on the side with a nice guy from the Russian Embassy."

"But seriously," the passenger said. "The latest is this. They're selling Ethel."

After a short pause, the informed spoke. Bill Burton said an amused, "Is that right?" Apple followed with a shocked, blurted, "That can't be true."

The passenger looked at him. "Of course it can. It is. She's old and finished. Worn out."

"But to sell her. My God. Think of all the good she's done for the various services over the years. Think of everything she's contributed."

"Sure, and in the process become known to every spook in the Western theatre of operations."

"That's accepted. It doesn't matter."

The passenger said, "It's time we got rid of her." He turned back to the window and started humming again.

Apple slumped in his seat slowly like a balloon with a leak. He felt exhausted with the callousness of it all. The brutality. The betrayal.

Ethel was a London taxi. She had been in government service for over three decades, during which she had done tours of duty with the Vice Squad, Narcotic, and Customs and Excise before being passed over to the Intelligence departments. From local pimps to international spies, everyone knew Ethel. At one time a group of NATO undercover agents with nothing better to do between drinks had made a bet as to who could locate her first; a Canadian won in two and a half hours and scratched his initials near the radiator. The letters USSR which were later found under the initials had been put there by a Hammer—a member of the KGB.

Retirement would be the proper thing, Apple mused plaintively. Surely they could afford to give Ethel a graceful old age, in a cozy garage, or perhaps among potted palms in an antique-vehicle museum. To sell her was too cruel.

Apple sat in his slump until aroused by Bill Burton asking, "Whereabouts in Kensington, old son?"

The United Kingdom Philological Institute had its home in a mansion, one whose elegance put to shame the mini-skyscrapers on every hand, like a mannered dowager among gawky debs. The marble-tiled hall had a curving staircase that might have been created especially for the heroine's big entrance in act one. It led up to a long corridor. Here, the necessary had abnegated the elegant. Plasterboard walls and plywood doors had been used to form a number of offices. One of these belonged to Apple.

He was sitting with his feet on the desk. Under his shoes lay the work he was supposed to be doing: a proofing job on the Institute's latest booklet, on Walloon. Instead, not uncommonly, Apple's thoughts were on espionage.

He was trying to imagine what sort of operation could be connected to the scene he had played a part in two hours ago. What caper was the passenger going to pull? And, was it to be in some far-flung exotic spot, or here in town, to do with the London Music Week?

For five days, the capital was hosting an ambitious and polynational festival of musical events—to several of which Apple had tickets. There were performers here from thirty-seven different countries. Visitors ranged from hundred-man symphony orchestras to soloists, just as styles went from jazz to chamber. Not for years had so many of the world's prestige artistes been gathered together in one city at the same time. It was an occasion in the grand manner.

Unusually, the Russians had not sent a mammoth such as the Red Army Choir, or a crowd of dancers from the Ukraine. As their representative they had chosen a quartet, four male singers of simple folk songs.

Even so, it was Moscow who was winning the greatest and purest propaganda from the festival. The Russian Rural Quartet earned the most headlines, gave the most interviews, signed the most autograph books, had the most exposure on television coverage of the London Music Week and drew the most public affection.

The four men were nonagenarians. The youngest was ninety years old, the oldest ninety-four. They were strapping men in robust health, even handsome in a decrepit sort of way, and had a pleasant manner. No one, critic or fan, minded that the four sang dreary songs in an unknown language and rarely got their voices to blend. They were the festival's acknowledged hit.

Moscow was delighted. Using no publicity, underplaying its contribution to the point of a no-comment, Russia was handing every other attending nation a generous face-loss. If Moscow did have any statement to make in the matter, it was the inferred:

Now look here. We don't know what the fuss is all about. In the Union of Soviet Socialist Republics there's nothing unusual about people of this age being hale and happy and gifted. Really now. Calm down.

Apple changed the cross of his ankles and nodded cannily. The folk singers were obviously of no interest to Intelligence, he mused. So if the coming caper had its base in London this week, the pertinent parties would have to be those from East Germany, or Poland, or . . .

Apple's thought-line was broken by noise from the street outside, the beep-honk-toot of jammed traffic. When the sound faded, Apple found himself dwelling on what he had been trying to avoid for the past two hours. In a thought-aside, he hoped it wouldn't keep him awake tonight.

Ethel. Poor Ethel.

Apple had a vision of her being sold to some awful youth, one of the punk generation, a lad with strange clothes, orange hair and five ear-rings in one ear. He cuts off Ethel's top to make a jagged convertible. He adds fancy fins. He paints her body pink and her tyres green and her radiator bright blue. He reduces her to an absurdity.

Apple closed his eyes. To cancel the vision of shame and degradation, he rapidly began to go through the various definitions of the word *punk,* ignoring the derivatives of the original American Indian term as being without piquancy.

A prostitute. A young hobo. A beginner. Anything worthless. An inexperienced assistant to a movie cameraman. A sexual urning in prison. A fairground . . .

The interruption this time was a voice. Close at hand, it said, "Ahem."

Apple sprang his eyes open. Standing in front of the desk was his superior, Professor Warden.

As Apple snapped his feet off the desk he was attacked by a blush. It was a bad one, a three-bell rampager, a sear that covered his whole body.

Apple fought back with his latest weapon. He did so while rising and making vague gestures of apology for his sloth, though he was unaware of these physical actions. His concentration needed to be intense and total in order for him to create the required picture. It formed.

He is in a large black cast-iron pot. The water is level with his chin. Steam rises to compete with the smoke that is drifting up from the fire below, the one that is heating the water. The cannibal chief is adding various herbs and salt, while his tribe stands around with hungry eyes.

According to the advertiser's claim, the heat would act to counter the blush, the fear would cancel its cause. Gratifyingly, it worked. Apple began to cool and calm. He let the picture go and smiled weakly.

Professor Warden said a worried, "You were quite red for a moment there, Porter."

An old, frail-seeming and bewildered-looking man, Warden spoke fourteen languages fluently but often had difficulty in finding the word he wanted in English.

"A slight case of high blood pressure," Apple said. His smile now was in self-congratulation for his inventiveness.

He wished he could let his dossier know. "That, you see, sir, is why I had my feet on the desk."

"Did you, my boy? I didn't notice."

"Oh. Well, I did. Sort of."

"You had your eyes closed," the old man said, demonstrating briefly. "Are you in—er—ah—?"

Apple suggested, "Trouble?"

"No, no. You're not in—um—?"

"Debt?"

"No, Porter," Professor Warden said. "Love. That's it. Have you fallen in it?" He nodded. "Again?"

"No, sir. Not in the least. I had my eyes closed out of respect for the perfection of this booklet. It's a real gem."

The old man nodded eagerly. "It is, isn't it? That's what I popped in now to see you about. I'm terribly glad you agree. It's a real—er—"

"Gem, professor?"

"No, my boy. Pleasure. It's a real pleasure to have someone with your feeling for language working with me at the Institute. But tell me, please, what did you think of the booklet's final section?"

Apple had nowhere reached that far. He was saved, however, by yet another interruption. Third time lucky, he thought when his telephone shrilled.

Professor Warden said, "I mustn't keep you from your work. We'll talk of this again." Nodding, smiling, he wandered out of the room as if not sure which way to go.

Apple sat in his chair and picked up the telephone receiver. He stood again at once when a plain brown voice asked, "Can you talk, Porter?"

Apple's pulses speeded up. He thought the repeat *third time lucky* while shaking his head. He said, "No, sir. Not with complete confidence."

"Why not?"

"The door's open."

From the other end of the line came a sigh, one of many in the Watkin repertoire. Apple had come across it before several times. It meant, he knew, that its creator was at the beginning of his tether.

Angus Watkin said, slowly, giving out words the way a bankrupt miser counts his fingers, "Then why, Porter, do you not go and close it?"

"Yes, sir," Apple said. "Hold on, please." He put the receiver down gently. During the four-stride trip across the room and back, he warned himself not to get excited. His chief could be calling with a rocket, a complaint that his neglected agent had done or said something wrong in the car this morning.

Apple lifted the receiver. "Right, sir. All clear."

"I do hope, Porter," Angus Watkin said, "that this is causing you no inconvenience."

The insult, for Apple, lay in the fact that his Control was hinting behind the sarcasm that said sarcasm would probably be too subtle to be detected by the listener. It was a shame, Apple thought, that Watkin had to be such an odious, unlikeable bastard.

He said, "No problem, sir. I wasn't doing anything of particular import."

"Then it's all right for me to proceed, I take it."

"It is, sir, yes."

"Fine," Angus Watkin said, the sarcasm lingering in his voice like a tired echo. "May I take it also that you will be available at noon?"

Apple was tempted to say he had a lunch date. He lacked the courage. "I'm free," he said.

There was a pause before Watkin tossed out lightly, "I have a little errand for you."

Apple stood straighter. "Errand" was spookspeak for an

Intelligence operation. With his pulses tripping faster, Apple again warned himself. This could be the result of what he had labelled a Porter-catch, which was the reverse of a Freudian-slip, and meant motivated mishearing. Often it had led him astray.

"Excuse me, sir," Apple said. "I'm not sure I got that right—what it is you have for me."

"Yes, you did, Porter. I would hardly be calling you for an exchange of pleasantries, would I?"

"No, sir. Hardly."

Angus Watkin said, "You might, of course, have had your own theories as to the reason for this call. What they could be I can't imagine."

Explain, that meant. Thinking quickly, Apple came up with, "I had the idea, sir, that you wanted to question me about the agent I met earlier today."

"In what area?"

"I really don't know. His appearance. His responses during the action. Perhaps, and more likely, something to do with his speech."

"No," Watkin said. "But as to the last, I dare say you caught the faint Swedish flavour in his accent."

Apple recognized the trap, one of the games his chief played for his own amusement. Watkin was obviously having a dull morning in his office, wherever that might be.

Apple said, "I must confess that I didn't, sir. But then, there wasn't a great deal of talk."

Angus Watkin grunted—and Apple realized that once again he had out-clevered himself. He ought to have allowed the trap to work. To stay on the best side of Watkin you needed to let him win every move.

"Come to think of it, though," Apple corrected, "and now that you mention it, I do seem to recall a certain amount of fierceness in the sibilants. But, as I said, there wasn't a great deal of talk."

"There is now, however," Angus Watkin said. His voice had become a shade brighter. "I have a cup of tea before me, and I am not one of those brilliant people who can drink and talk at the same time. May I conclude, Porter?"

"Certainly, sir."

"I shall say this once and once only. Understood?"

"Understood, sir. I'm ready to absorb."

"At twenty minutes past twelve precisely," Angus Watkin said, "you will exit by the front entrance of that place in which you are employed. You will head north. Soon you will see, on the opposite side of the street, heading in the same direction as yourself, a Japanese gentleman who has the stamp of the tourist. Neck-slung cameras, casual clothes, map in hand. Clear?"

"Perfectly, sir."

"On the unlikely chance of there being another Japanese tourist in the same state of dress and perambulation, you will know your mark by the fact that, with the aforementioned map, he alternately slaps his right thigh and his left shoulder." Watkin paused. "It's all good espionage stuff, wouldn't you say, Porter?"

Even while knowing it was absurd for a grown man to put out his tongue, Apple put out his tongue. Retracting it, he risked displeasure by ignoring the question and asking one of his own: "What next, sir?"

"Nothing. Stay back and on your own side of the street. You will be led to where you have to be."

"And that's all, sir?"

"It is. Good morning." The line clicked to deadness.

After putting the receiver back in its cradle, Apple sank slowly into his chair. He felt feeble. It was, he knew, the weakness of shock, which had arrived now that his pulses had settled and he had accepted that he was actually going to be sent out on a mission.

And a mission of consequence, Apple mused dazedly. "A little errand," Angus Watkin had said. He wouldn't have used that particular adjective unless he had meant the reverse. Although, yes, he might have used it simply because he knew or hoped that it would be given a different interpretation. With Angus Watkin you never could be sure. If he were ever to put all his cards on the table, they'd be still in the packet.

Apple got up. To bring himself alert he began to do deep knee-bends. His mind cleared.

He realized now that of course, *of course,* the caper had to be connected with this morning's car incident. Watkin's call coming right on top of that was too fantastic a coincidence for it to be otherwise. So what was it all about?

Apple stopped the knee-bends and shook his head. He told himself that it didn't matter, that whichever/whatever, big/small, a mission it was, and even if it turned out to be of no real import it would still be some kind of service involvement, as well as helping to keep his mind off Ethel.

The street was noontime busy when Apple left the building at twenty minutes past twelve. He was precise to the second, after having stood in the entrance hall for the previous seven minutes, the last of which he spent staring at his watch.

Apple went down the front steps and turned right. He was facing roughly north. His walk had to it the saunter of a man who has nothing particular to do during his lunch break, and an hour and a half to not do it in. Apple was aping other office escapees, in keeping with the Training Three adage relating to herdmanship, *Copy the majority.*

Before fifty yards had been covered, Apple spotted the mark he had to dog. Stout, bulge-necked, the man wore colourful sports clothes, a cap and three cameras. Frequently he glanced aside, which allowed a view of his oriental features. With a folding of paper he was tapping his right leg.

Apple smiled inside as he followed, keeping on his own side of the street. He was enjoying the details.

As Angus Watkin knew, and had snidely dropped during the telephone call, Apple had a romantic view of the espionage world. That was what had led him to become a part of the undercover services, rather than a burning desire to serve his country. In his favourite fiction reading he avoided the warts-and-all, kitchen-sink variety; avoided dwelling on dirty tricks, double-crosses, real or figurative stabs in the back, treachery as a commonplace; avoided the true in preference for what ought to be. The spy game was as decent as cricket, Apple liked to believe. That it was as complex as chess he knew with pleasure for an absolute. He loved the frills and cunning moves, held warmly to the symbol of the agent waiting calmly under a lamppost on a midnight corner, adored the ego-sooth of belonging to a highly select society of men, and loved, as does everyone, the fact of being in on a secret.

Apple saw the glamour, ignored the dirt.

So he was titillated, not alarmed, when he got the sensation across his shoulders. It was as if a line were being traced there by a sensuous forefinger. His flesh was telling him that he, the follower, was being followed.

The sensation quickly faded, then returned for another short stretch after a pause, which increased Apple's intrigued interest. The tailer was a pro. He knew that his attention would be sensed by someone else in the same business if he watched the upper body for too long and therefore was observing in spates.

Apple thought it unlikely that the person behind was a casual, meaning someone merely looking at an unusually tall man. In such an event, the stare would have to be prolonged in order to provoke the trailing finger.

Which came and went over the next ten minutes as Apple stayed behind his mark. The Japanese quasi-tourist strolled, gazed about sightseeingly and sometimes tapped the map against his left shoulder.

Apple resisted the urge to look back, even though he knew all the acceptable methods.

One, pretend interest in a car that's going by. Two, exchange greetings in passing with an invented person in a shop doorway and keep it up while walking on semi-backwards. Three, bump into someone and turn to apologize. Four, stop abruptly and start retracing your steps, doing the same after a moment with an oh-never-mind shake of the head. Five, stop a passer-by to ask the way but act as if it's you who has been stopped.

Trouble was, Apple thought, all the acceptables were known to everyone in the trade. They were a give-away. In any case, he was going to follow instructions to the letter. He had no orders to investigate occurrences.

That give-away thought, it made Apple feel superior to the person behind. Himself, if he were tailing, he would look only at the legs. They were insensitive to attention—so long as the mark was male.

Apple arrived on Kensington Gore. The wide road was a hustle of traffic. The Japanese started across. He made it to the other side in wild fits and untidy starts, his cameras swinging. Looking ruffled, he fanned himself with the map.

Well, you made an honourable balls of that, Apple thought cheerfully. He waited for the traffic to show a gap, which he entered in cool style, and then had to race as cars came tearing up on the other lane. Safely arrived, he twisted his neck in his collar and smiled falsely.

The Japanese had gone into the edging trees of Hyde

Park. Apple followed as if prepared to be bored. Once among the trunks and tall bushes, hidden, he halted and peered back through the foliage.

He was disappointed to see no one who stood out as a tail. That is, of the fifty-odd people within the necessary range, on the far side and this, any single one could have been the shadow. It would take at least a minute to pick out the right one, Apple reasoned. And he was falling back.

Glancing around, Apple saw that the Japanese was still in sight among the people who were strolling in the park. There was time, Apple thought as he turned back to face the road; time to see who it was that followed this way.

Pedestrians here were going straight on by. From the other side, moving together through a traffic gap, came three men. They were average types. They reached the middle line, where they were held by a steady stream of cars.

Apple's glance back turned into a look when he saw there was no sign of the Japanese mark. After hesitating for some seconds, Apple returned to his watch through the foliage. He couldn't resist the peep, which he failed to recognize as the fundamental act of spying.

One of the three men made it to safety with a burst of sprinting. He turned and went towards a bus-stop. The other two men waited, one impatiently, jiggling his fists as if they held coins.

Apple felt like doing the same. He kept glancing behind, although there was nothing to see but strangers. Come on, he willed. Let's go.

As traffic eased, the men strode across to this side. One went left, the other right, and neither showed the slightest interest in the direction Apple had taken.

He couldn't wait any longer, to see if anyone else appeared in long-distance pursuit. He could have been mistaken in the first place.

Apple swung around and started running. He dodged between the noontimers who were ambling or standing in groups, sprawling on the grass or sitting with sandwiches. He ran tall. It was one of those rare occasions when he blessed his height. Not a single head blocked his view.

Apple cut around a group, leapt a sprawler. Stiff-legged, he brought himself down in speed on at last seeing his mark. The Japanese was near at hand, although moving ahead at a strong, purposeful march, as if implacably bent on the next step in his tour itinerary.

His worry settling, Apple followed when the gap had grown bigger. He was led across the park and onto the Bayswater Road and along to Notting Hill Gate. At no time did he get that trailing-finger sensation, nor did it come while he and his mark, after crossing the main road at pedestrian lights, went into quiet residential streets. It had been a mistake, Apple accepted. A casual.

That Pater Road was the end of the line Apple knew by the Japanese mock-tourist's actions. Not only did he tap the name-plate of the street in passing, he also let the briskness go out of his body.

It was a street of small, cheerless, detached villas, each with the minimum of garden at front and skinny sides. Circa 1920, the houses looked like the homes of people who had gone into retailing in a small way, and failed.

At the gate of a villa two thirds of the way along, the Japanese stopped. After glancing around at the desertion, he looked directly at Apple, slanted his head briefly to one side, towards the house, turned and walked on. Apple had the strong impression that he would never see him again.

The front door was three yards of crazy-paving from the gate. The miniature, man-height poplars that edged the path appeared faintly ridiculous in their attempt to create the impression of an approach. Apple sympathized.

He pressed the bell that lay under number eighteen. The door opened at once, which meant the existence of a peephole. Apple wasn't surprised to see a familiar face, though he had somehow expected that it would belong to Bill Burton.

The man was middle-aged and of meagre stature. His eyes and cheeks were sunken, as though he read a lot, while not eating. Grey, his hair was so sparse that it grew fluffy in bluff. He wore a woollen muffler, the blue coveralls of a mechanic, white running shoes.

Age and build and face were misleading, as Apple was aware. The last time they had met, the man, known as Albert, had held Apple helpless with a two-finger grip.

Standing aside, Albert said, "Come in. It's that door at the end." His accent was cockney. "And don't forget to knock."

"I know my party manners, thank you."

"What's the weather like up there?"

"By Jove," Apple drawled as he passed, "I haven't heard that one before."

"Is that a fact now? Well, well. It's as old as the hills."

Another voice was heard. Languorous and dull, it said, "*When* you two have finished with your banter."

Albert said, "Yes, sir." Apple said, "Sorry, sir." He went on along the passage, towards its end doorway, in which stood Angus Watkin.

His average suit was averagely neat, averagely wrinkled; his ordinary shirt had an ordinary tie with an ordinary knot; his body was standard height and slightly overweight to the standard degree.

Aged between fifty and sixty, he had a face as unremarkable as his neat brown hair. The eyes seemed sleepy, not intelligent. All in all, Angus Watkin looked like that man who always stands alone at the bar because no one finds him interesting enough to talk to.

"Tea, Albert," he said, retreating.

Apple followed into a small study. It was furnished with an eye to bleakness. The lights were on, the drapes drawn. Playing at winter, a coal fire burned in the hearth, facing which were two armchairs with high backs.

Obeying a casual gesture, Apple took one chair while his chief took the other. Angus Watkin leaned back and put his fingertips together as though they were cracked egg-shells. He asked blandly:

"Were you followed, Porter?"

Which, Apple guessed, meant that he had been, and that Watkin knew about it. He nodded. "I got that impression, sir. At least, as far as the park." In the name of good fellow-agent relations he amended, "But I could've been mistaken."

"You were not. I had some of my people keep a watch on the procedure." With Watkin it was always *my*, never *our*. "I thought it wouldn't hurt to see how confidential my telephone call to you had been. To see, in fine, if you were followed by anyone unauthorized."

Apple grudgingly gave him a ten for thoroughness. "I understand, sir." But next, with a flash of despair, he wondered if this whole matter was simply a Watkin way of checking telephone security in respect of his minions. The same routine could be going on with scores of other people.

Watkin said, "You were not followed, I'm pleased to say. It is, therefore, prudent to continue."

Apple sagged like someone released from a brace. Over Angus Watkin's forehead passed a movement that could have been a frown. He asked:

"Are you fretting for a cigarette, Porter?"

The question came at the same second as Apple got a

craving for the post-crisis smoke. The man's a bloody genius, he thought while nodding.

"Odious habit," Angus Watkin said. "But indulge it if you must." He glanced at the curtained window. "Have the goodness to blow your smoke towards the fireplace."

By the time Apple was taking his first, luxurious drag, Albert had tapped and entered. He went out again after depositing a tray on the low table near his chief's elbow. Angus Watkin poured.

"It's two sugars, isn't it, Porter?"

"Please," Apple said, thinking: I bet he knows what size shoes I take. Bet he knows everything about me—except Monico. Apple smiled. "Yes, sir. Two sugars."

When Watkin passed over the cup and saucer, he said, "This, as you will have surmised, is a safe-house. There are several spread around in London and its suburbs, apart from the country places. The Russians know of some one third of them. It stays fairly constant at that, even though there is a regular change—leaving old houses, getting new. Number Eighteen Pater Road the Soviets do not know about."

Apple, who had been hoping he would be asked the name of the street, said a polite, "I see, sir."

"We're using this place for a while because the Russians, as we know, and they know that we know, are also familiar with the various HQ buildings which are part of what some of you people refer to as Upstairs."

Apple nodded. He mused that his Control was being unusually expansive today.

Angus Watkin leaned back with his cup and saucer. After a single, delicate sip he said, "Should anything untoward occur this week, the first place the KGB would rush to would be those buildings. Hence the use of this safe-house."

Apple blew out a long stream of smoke in the direction

of the hearth. He made his chief happy and eased the way for himself, by asking the expected:

"What do you mean, sir—untoward?"

"That which the Russians do not like. For my part, of course, it would be not the untoward but the felicitous. And I shall be here at that time—indeed, all the time—in order to accept the gift."

"Gift, sir?"

"Gift, Porter. The one which you will bring me."

Apple gave more happiness by saying, honestly, "I'm afraid I don't understand, sir."

Angus Watkin hummed faintly while taking several judicious sips of his tea. He went back to drinking after the order, "Tell me what you know about the Soviet contribution to the London Music Week."

Apple told. It didn't take long, even though he padded it by giving a physical description of the Russian Rural Quartet, recalling press photographs and television shots. Each singer was tall and sinewy, had flowing white hair and a droopy white moustache, a brown face of strong features. The four wore normal clothes off-stage, dressed peasant-style on.

"Well done, Porter," Watkin said.

Apple was so surprised at the praise that he let a cloud of smoke go billowing free. He chased it with sweeping wafts of his arm, and condemned it by throwing his cigarette in the fire.

Angus Watkin put down his cup and saucer. "Now tell me this," he said. "What, in your opinion, would be the worst that could happen this week as far as the Soviet Union is concerned?"

Apple shook his head. He suggested, "Laryngitis?"

"No, Porter."

"Some other kind of illness or problem that would prevent the Quartet performing?"

"No, Porter."

"Then I have no idea, sir," Apple said. He wasn't merely playing the flatterer.

Angus Watkin again carefully built a steeple with his fingers. He said, "The Soviet Union is making a massive amount of propaganda hay while its sons shine here this week. Even people who are not musically inclined are aware of the four old singers. They are an international hit, a global phenomena. They are also national heroes in their own country and have been for seventy years. Russia has never had an advertisement so convincing, so potent."

Watkin nodded head and hands with perfect timing. "The very worst thing imaginable that could befall the Soviet Union at this time, a mammoth loss of face, would be for one of the singers to defect."

Apple reached his cup and saucer to the tray. Back upright he said, "I can see that, sir, but surely . . ."

"Surely such a thing is unlikely? Yes, very. The men are extremely old. In Moscow they live in what there passes for luxury. They want for nothing. They are large fish. Adulation is constantly theirs. Behind the Iron Curtain they come and go as they wish. Agreed?"

"Yes, sir."

"In short, there is no reason whatever why they should want to leave their motherland. If they did, it could only be seen by the world as meaning that the aforementioned motherland was not worth living in, no matter whosoever one might happen to be. Agreed again?"

"Agreed, sir. It'd be the biggest blow to Moscow since the defection of Nureyev. But he did do it, sir, despite having all the same perks and glamour in Russia that the singers have."

"He, however, had many years of life ahead of him. What would a man of ninety-odd want with the West?"

"Nothing. Nothing at all. So yes, defection is not only unlikely but implausible."

Angus Watkin almost smiled, with one side of his mouth. Slowly he leaned forward. "Porter," he said, "you are going to kidnap one of those singers."

CHAPTER 2

See how easy that was?

Bill Burton's question came back often to Apple as he walked home to Bloomsbury. The journey he took at a plod. His surroundings were lost on him. He was gloomy. Not even the realization that the droop at knee, hip, shoulder and neck had rendered him several degrees shorter would have brought him cheer. Apple was low.

At the apartment, his return of Monico's frisky greeting was muted. Casual pats took the place of the daily wrestling match. With a cool sniff Monico went to his armchair in the living-room.

Apple telephoned the United Kingdom Philological Institute. To Professor Warden he reported that he had just seen his doctor, who advised a week's rest to bring down the blood pressure. The old man said:

"Take off as much time as you—er—"

"Thank you very much, professor," Apple said dully. "Good afternoon."

Next Apple went and flopped himself down on his bed, which was two feet longer than the standard. When he stopped bouncing, he stared at the ceiling while recalling the last of the interview in Pater Road.

Angus Watkin had told him where the Soviet visitors were staying; their sightseeing schedule would probably be available later. He had given him the safe-house's telephone number to memorize and had said that he could ask for almost any help he wanted.

"The point of the operation, of course," Angus Watkin had said, "is that no one outside of a few of my people will know that the singer has been abducted. It will be given out that he has defected, asked for political asylum. Perhaps I shall be able to arrange for him to give a press conference, at which he could make a statement to that effect."

Apple had nodded numbly and dumbly. Anything, he felt sure, could be rigged by Watkin and the Upstairs experts.

"Such a defection, Porter, as you are aware, would shatter a vast hole in the Soviet propaganda, which is my aim." Watkin rose. "And that is all for the moment. Your number-name in this operation is One. Good day, Porter."

Not even remembering his position cheered Apple. He had never been a One before. Now, he wished he was a Fifty.

Apple got off the bed. After removing jacket and shoes, he put on his robe and his slippers with the paper-thin soles. He felt no better. Going to the living-room he began pacing, the act a slouch.

"I ought to have turned the job down," Apple told Monico. "I suppose I was too bewildered. I wasn't quite taking it all in. Thank you, sir, but no thank you, sir, that's what I should've said."

Monico sat in his usual position, chin high, ears pricked, front legs crossed and paws dangling off the edge of the seat. His head swung ponderously back and forth as he followed the pacer with his eyes.

"The thing is," Apple said, "I can't do it. Oh, don't get me wrong. Let's have no misunderstandings. I don't mean in respect of mechanics. The job itself is, I suppose, pull-able-off. Bill Burton and team made that clear this morning. And that's only one of many methods."

Monico started on a yawn. He was used to these monologues. They were generally about the latest girl-friend, but to Monico they all sounded the same. He ended his yawn, as always, with a faint squeak.

After shooting his dog a reproachful glance, Apple said, "No, I can't do it. It wouldn't be right. How can I prevent a man from returning to his country, his home, his family? How can I contrive to condemn him to permanent exile? That would be a terrible thing to do, even to an enemy, and I haven't even met these men. These poor old men who're having a wonderful time in the late evening of their lives."

Stopping, Apple faced Monico and spread his arms. "So you see, it's no go. I can't do it. No, no, don't give me any arguments. The kidnap I definitely cannot and will not do, so don't waste your breath."

Monico clopped his mouth, blinked, lowered his head to the crossed legs. His eyes began to glaze.

"I refuse to discuss the matter," Apple said. "The subject of an abduction is permanently finished." He went to the mantelpiece, got a cigarette and lit up. Smoke sprayed in a curve as he suddenly swung around, an arm pointing at Monico, whose eyes were now closed.

"However," Apple said, "perhaps all isn't totally lost. Maybe there's something else I can do as a form of salvage, so that bloody Angus Watkin won't cross me off his list for good and always. Which is what would happen if I called in now and backed out of the job. It's too late for that."

Apple stabbed a forefinger at the sleeping dog. "There's nothing wrong with failure, after all. Not every operation that's mounted ends with success, not by a long chalk, not even when the top pros are involved. I needn't go into details. We all know about those big flops. So failure here won't be the end of me."

After taking two deep drags on his cigarette, Apple threw it behind him into the dead fireplace. He showed Monico spread hands while saying:

"But I'm not without brains. Surely I can come up with an answer to the problem. There must be a way around it. I'll have to give it a good think."

Which, Apple told himself as he moved away from the hearth, was to treat himself to his favourite food. It had rarely failed to work.

Apple strode to the kitchen. Within ten minutes he was sitting at the table with a pot of tea and a plate of toast. The toast had a thick layer of butter under the thick layer of marmalade, which was lemon flavour.

Seconds after Apple's first loud-crunching mouthful, Monico came into the room. He sat nearby. Alternately, he whined and shivered. He disliked marmalade, whatever the flavour might be, and if given a tidbit would decline to eat it; but, his owner had figured, he felt obliged to play the part that was expected of him. Apple approved. He was all for the social niceties.

At a steady pace Apple crunched on, with sips of tea between slices. He felt safe and coddled, like a boy being pampered by Mum following some outdoor strife. His mind worked quietly at the problem, proceeding without haste.

Giving up on the shivering and whining, point made, Monico got up and left the kitchen.

Apple poured more tea—as a delayer. He had reached the last slice of toast but one and had found only two possible solutions, neither of which would be acceptable.

The first was to go ahead with the operation as desired by Angus Watkin, actually pull a kidnap job on one of the folk singers, and then to allow him to get free. The old man, however, though fit, might not be fit enough for that much physical effort, and Watkin might sneakily pounce before the escape could be managed.

The second idea was to abduct some ancient and innocent Englishman, take him to the safe-house, then allow it to be discovered that a sad mistake had been made. Mistake, however, was considered by Upstairs to be worse than failure, and the whole scheme was dishonest in the first place.

Apple bit into the penultimate slice of toast. He chewed like winces, his eyebrows wistful. It wasn't until he had swallowed the last overchewed piece and was about to send his tongue in search of crumbs that he finally found the answer. He closed his eyes in pride and relief.

Ten seconds of that was enough. Eyes alertly open, smiling, Apple picked up the last piece of toast. He masticated perkily and put his idea in clear perspective.

He would choose one of the four folk singers. He would see as much of him as he could. He would gain his confidence. He would sell him a marvellous picture of life in the West. And, finally, he would try to *persuade* him to defect.

The west central branch of the British Communist Party had its office in a defunct shop, which stood in a semi-demolished street, which lay in a decaying district. According to the lettering still visible through a coat of paint, the business had once belonged to a butcher. That seemed to go with the predominance of red among the books and pamphlets and slogans displayed in the grimy window. Even the price-tags were crimson, a gory detail.

Apple unbuttoned his jacket, loosened his tie, made his hair slightly ruffled. Now, he told himself, he looked your regular proletarian. Certainly he felt less a member of the Establishment—to which, in any case, he belonged only by association.

Apple's true political home lay somewhere between the poles, on an equator of whose exact location he was never quite sure. If he thought about it too much he got a headache. If he eeled out of thinking about it he got embarrassed. He rarely thought about it.

Using a labourer's swagger, Apple entered the shop, which had a smell of sawdust, old aprons and the cheaper cuts. The decor was a repeat of the window display, the furniture was a trestle-table.

Apple gave himself full marks for this idea of his. To form an immediate rapport with whichever of the four old men he would decide on, he would approach him with Communist literature, pretending the while to be unaware that the man was, in fact, a Russian national, one of the visiting Rural Quartet.

A woman came in from the rear. Middle-aged, she was pink and agitated, as if she'd just got off a train on which she'd been squashed between fellow travellers.

"Good afternoon," she said in a vaguely threatening manner. "Better Red than dead."

"Oh, quite," Apple said.

Across from him, the woman leaned forward on the table. "Do you know who the world's five most widely distributed authors are?"

As it happened, Apple did. He chanted happily, "Lenin, Stalin, Shakespeare, Erskine Caldwell and Enid Blyton."

The woman beamed. Fondly she said, "Comrade."

With an inner scoff at the short-sightedness of REMARKS in condemning his affection for odd data, Apple said, "Thank you." He decided not to mention that the works of the first two authors were given away rather than sold. He doubted if it would help.

The woman asked with wide-eyed goodwill, "How can I be of service to you, comrade?"

"I'd like some literature, please," Apple said. "To fit in my pocket. Stuff I can hand out as I go along. Fight the good fight, you know. Now is the time for all good men, and so forth. It pays to advertise."

By the time Apple had finished speaking, the woman had come around the trestle-table. From it she began to lift printed matter, which she thrust into Apple's arms. There were books, pamphlets, handbills, newspapers—some in singles, some in roped stacks six inches high.

With the weight of the growing pile pulling him forward, Apple protested mildly that a little sampling was what he had meant, a mere hint of the better life, an appetizer or two to get folk interested.

"It does the heart good," the woman said, loading, loading. "Wait till I tell Fred."

Accepting a final stack, clamping it into place with his chin, Apple sidled towards the door. He smiled an impersonation of kindness at the woman as, following him, she listed the names of the people she couldn't wait to tell.

Nodding sideways at Jim and Ethel and good old Percy, Apple got through the door and set off along the street. He gave a final nod to the call of, "Farewell, comrade."

Ethel, he thought.

He came level with the inset doorway of a boarded-up shop. Already holding a quantity of rubbish, it would be the perfect place to get rid of the major part of his load.

In moving towards the doorway, Apple craned a look behind. The woman was watching, smiling. She waved and called out, "Get a taxi." Apple nodded again and went on.

Ethel, he thought.

He reached a corner. Rounding it quickly, he strode on in answer to the urgency of the growing ache in his arms. He almost ran the last yards to the mouth of an alley, which he entered at a steadier pace on seeing the garbage cans. By one of these he set his load down.

It was only a minute's work to separate from the pile a dozen or so pamphlets. Slipping them easily into his pockets, he rose and went back to the street.

Where he stopped. Apple stopped and let the whole thought come into comfortable place. If Ethel was for sale, why couldn't he buy her himself?

Apple went to a snack bar to consider methods of tracing. Over coffee and a desperate doughnut he concluded that (A), he could not, now, being on a mission, have it known that he had interests elsewhere; that (B), using official channels was ruled out by A; that (C), he could probably manage the task through connections of his own.

Apple used the snack-bar telephone. He made four calls. The first was to an ex-girl-friend who was second secretary to a fingers-in-pies businessman. Apple asked what happened when government vehicles needed to be sold. The girl said to ask somebody who knew something about cars.

The second call was to Apple's local mechanic, who advised trying the National Automobile Association.

The third call, to an acquaintance who worked as doorman at the NAA building, brought the information that disposition was handled by the Ministry of Works.

The fourth call went to another old girl-friend, member of the typing pool at the MoW. She said that all wheeled property was sent to the Works storage garage in East Hackney.

Whistling cheerfully, Apple left the snack-bar. He reflected that, as the sharpies say, it ain't what you know, but who.

A vacant cab came along. Apple hailed it, got in and gave his destination. Settling back, he realized the why of his cheer. It was more than simply having the opportunity to do something humane about Ethel, he mused. It was because he knew, knew under his veneer of confidence, that the folk-singer operation had little hope of success, via persuasion. He was merely going through the motions, grabbing at a straw that would never be even near a camel. So it was doubly important to him to triumph with a coup of buying Ethel.

Cheered still more on account of his neat self-analysis, Apple felt better about the Russian operation. He thought he had a good chance of bringing it off.

The cab stopped outside a long, low building. Painted dull grey, it looked like a home for retired convicts. Apple paid the driver and went in.

Stone steps led him up to an office. Its farther wall was made of glass, giving a view of a vast garage. Spread out below were vehicles of all types, including buses, trucks and horse-drawn carriages.

Not fully aware of his immediate surroundings, Apple stood looking down onto the jumble of closely set roofs. His eyes darted from one patch of black to another. None, as far as he could judge, had the right shape.

Now taken by nervous excitement, Apple turned. He saw a dozen desks, only one of which had an occupant, who was also the only other person in the room. Bald and squat, a sour-looking forty, the man was engrossed in reading.

Telling himself with another part of his mind that there was no need to feel guilty about having thrown away the Communist literature, no matter how much it had cost to produce, that it was certainly not a sort of book-burning, Apple crossed to the occupied desk. He cleared his throat.

Not glancing up, the man said, "We're closed."

Apple said, "The door's open."

"We're closed."

Apple leaned down on the desk. His impression was that he was behaving courteously. He didn't know about his drumming fingers, the thrust of his head or the anxiously frowning grimness of his features.

"This is important," he said loudly.

Putting one hand on top of his baldness, the man looked up. He winced at the visitor's height and manner, leaned away and asked, "What?"

"Ethel," Apple said. "I mean a taxi. Where is it?"

"You want a taxi?"

"No, no. Not to ride in. One that's here. Or ought to be. Have you got a London cab down there? Thirty years old, buckled back bumper, dents on—"

"Closed," the man said with a twisted, humouring smile. "We give no information when we're closed." He rested both hands on the desk edge to ease himself farther backwards. "Sir."

Apple snapped, "I merely wish to know if she's here or not, and if she is, where she is exactly, and if she isn't, where I would go to find her."

"Oh yes."

"She's here?"

With a swift, agile movement the man got up and swung around so that he was standing behind his chair. He appeared to be torn between alarm and suspicion. Putting the hand back on top of his baldness he said, "No information. Against the rules. We're closed."

Apple pushed himself sternly upright. "In that case, I'll have a look for myself." He moved away, heading for a door in the glass wall.

In a high-climbing voice the man protested, "You can't do that alone."

"Please don't trouble yourself to show me the way," Apple said. He meant it as a politeness, but it sounded like the most virulent type of sarcasm.

"Stop or I'll press the bell."

Apple did stop, by the door. He looked around imperiously. "I beg your pardon?"

The man was back beside his desk, in a crouch, a forefinger poised. "I'll press it if you don't leave at once," he said. "This alarm bell. The security guards'll come running from all over the place."

Apple stared. Slowly he absorbed the words, understood the warning. His tension eased. He realized that either the man was mistaking him for someone else, had the issue confused, or was mentally unbalanced.

With a wide smile, blinking boyishly, Apple gave it a soothing try. "I'm just looking for a taxi, old chap."

The man made circles with his finger. "I'll press it, I'll press it."

"Perhaps if I explained about Ethel."

"You must leave. At once."

Unbalanced, Apple decided. And far enough gone to actually bring guards charging in, which could prove awkward at this particular time.

"At once. Do you hear?"

Apple bowed. "Certainly. Of course. Excuse me for bothering you." Giving the man a smile of compassion, he crossed to the exit. "Good afternoon."

It was only when he had gone down the steps, was pushing his way through the swing doors, which had glass in their upper halves, that Apple saw the real answer to the man's strange behaviour.

Apple's reflection in the glass told him that he was still in his proletarian role. Sighing at himself for the forgetfulness, the amateurism, he admitted that this was what came of mixing private and professional matters, of diluting his concentration.

On the street, Apple quickly combed his hair, then put straight the knot in his tie. While buttoning his jacket, he heard a bolt click into place behind him.

He shrugged and walked on. For the time being, he

thought, he would have to devote himself to the folk-singer operation. Ethel must be put out of mind. Also literature.

An hour later, back home, Apple called in. The number he dialled was the one he had been given earlier to memorize, not that of Upstairs. The rest was standard. The six digits he quoted to the answering voice identified both himself and the person he wished to contact. A moment later a familiar drone came on the line.

Apple said, "Good afternoon, sir. I'd like to put in a request, if that's all right."

"I told you it was, Porter," Angus Watkin said. "What do you want?"

"Transportation, please."

"By that, one imagines, you infer a car."

"Yes, sir."

Watkin gave a mid-scale sigh. "Why do you not simply obtain one from a hire firm? Getting expenses back from Accounts isn't quite as difficult as some of you people make out."

Apple smiled. He loved it when his superior was wrong. He said, "The problem is, sir, I might have a hard time getting the right colour."

"You have a particular shade in mind, Porter?"

"Red, sir. Bright red."

There followed a silence. Apple knew better than to suppose that Angus Watkin was surprised at the insane-sounding request for the pretty as opposed to the customary plain; the silence meant that he was swiftly trying to fathom motive, so he could comment on it before having it given to him.

Apple smiled again, now at hearing a faint bleakness in his chief's, "Yes, I see."

"Would that be possible, sir?" This was risky, an outright impertinence: all things were possible for Angus Watkin, preached Angus Watkin.

However, he punished merely by ignoring the question and asking, "When would you like it delivered?"

"No hurry, sir. In the morning will be fine."

"You feel no urgency, Porter?"

"In the matter of the car, sir, no."

"So be it," Angus Watkin said. "Now let's move to the matter of personnel."

It sobered Apple that he wasn't able to ask for assisting agents. Especially, he would have liked a female back-up, someone young, tall, attractive, mysterious and sophisticated. But colleagues would quickly realize that he had no intentions of working the snatch.

Briefly it passed through Apple's understanding that he was his own worst enemy. Why couldn't he be a little harder, just this once?

He said, "No personnel, sir. Thank you. I'm working this caper completely on my own."

"Caper," Angus Watkin said, as if it were the name of a cheap brand of tea. He hated slang. "But I mustn't take up any more of your time, must I?"

"Well, sir . . ."

"Goodbye, Porter."

Apple waited until a click told him that the line was dead before he allowed himself a slanderous, disgusting and atrocious thought about Angus Watkin. Ashamed of his cowardice, he put down the receiver politely and went at a morose pace to his bedroom.

While changing into his track suit, Apple got away from himself. He became lost in a daydream about that female back-up he couldn't have.

After successfully abducting all four folk singers, who are locked in the dungeon of a crumbling castle, he is in the bedchamber tending to the wounds received by Anastasia in their running gun-battle with the KGB. He has to cut away her clothes. He does so slowly and gently, while she, looking beautiful despite the smudge of dirt on one cheek, huskily thanks him for saving her life. She tells him that freckles are a sign of virility, tells him that height is everything, tells him in a whisper, "You're all man, One."

Later, Apple got Monico out of the building without trouble. He left by the front way, as always in the evening, for Charles Lampton then was often pottering in the backyard. Running, Apple had a visitation of his usual fret about having to leave the flat door open while he was gone. It didn't last long. He didn't need it tonight. He was all man.

The North London suburb lay three miles out. Apple jogged and walked. The journey was uneventful, even to the extent of Monico not being chased by one or more cats.

Gradually the residential streets got wider and quieter. Privet hedges and cast-iron railings were mostly replaced by high walls with seedlings of broken glass on top. Oaks stood like giant beggars along the kerbs. There were no parked cars and few moving.

Apple could see the name on the gateposts from a hundred yards away. He was on the opposite side of the street from Peace Manor. Above the wall he could see only trees, nothing of the house, which, Angus Watkin had said, had been loaned to the Russian visitors by one of those Anglo-Soviet friendship societies.

Coming level with the gateway, Apple stopped beside a tree. The gates were closed. Beyond them the house was visible in part at the end of a long driveway, a Georgian mansion in rich brown brick.

Apple stepped behind the tree trunk as a man strolled into view. He was on the other side of the gates of Peace Manor. About thirty, he had a pale face and a ski-jump nose. Apple knew him for a Russian by the unmistakable signs: schoolboy haircut, long upper lip, high shoulders on his suit.

The man was a low-scale Hammer, Apple decided. He thought about it.

After looking boredly both ways along the street, peering through the bars like a warder on his day off, the man wandered off and out of sight.

Apple also left, jogging back the way he had come. He was still thinking about it.

The wall would be tricky, bad in daylight and worse at night. Certainly Gateman would be armed, as would any other guards within the grounds. Covert action was therefore not advisable. The approach ought to be full frontal and with a flourish.

Nodding, Apple broke into a loping run. Monico came past, at a charge, as though he thought that the change in direction had been deliberate and wanted to show that he hadn't been fooled.

Soon, expensive living left behind, the pair were back among noise, bustle, commerce and homes with gainable doors; back, too, among the occasional catcall, source being those who fear the sight of a healthy action.

Apple came to a row of billboards. Each had an announcement, with photograph, pertaining to an event of the London Music Week. One picture was of a girl with long hair and a stern but pretty face. Stopping, Apple gazed up at Anna Schmidt.

She was a pianist. Aged twenty-four, she had escaped two years ago from East Berlin, after the death of her mother, who had been a noted pianist herself and Anna's teacher. Anna was a rabid anti-Communist, lived in Canada and often performed for charity.

Apple, who had a ticket for the Schmidt concert, was already smitten by Anna. He didn't know if this stemmed from her prettiness, her ethos, her musical gift or her dramatic dash to freedom on a bicycle at a Berlin checkpoint.

He so strongly suspected the last that he concluded it must be the first. When, running on, he drifted back into his back-up girl daydream, he used Anna's face on Anastasia.

"You're a hard man to wake up, One. I've been ringing you for half an hour."

"I wasn't asleep. I've been out."

"Not by the front door, you haven't."

"Skylight," Apple said.

It was a little before eight o'clock in the morning. Apple, back from the early outing with Monico, had been drying off from a shower when the telephone had rung. He and the caller, a stranger, had exchanged signals as if it were a competition in who could sound the most bored.

"I'm fond of a joke myself," the agent said. "But I'll stifle my laughter at your skylight gag and tell you that there's a present for you downstairs. To the left along the street."

"Thanks. I'll be down in ten minutes."

"Sooner, if you can. I haven't had my breakfast yet."

Apple pretended not to hear that. It didn't fit with the image he held dear of all who were involved in espionage. Subconsciously, Apple wanted operatives to have no need of food, dentists, handkerchiefs or bathrooms.

He said, "Yes, five or ten minutes."

Seven and a half minutes later, Apple emerged from Harlequin Mansions and went to the left. Ahead among the kerb-parked cars he could see a splash of bright red. Closer, he recognized the car as a four-door Mazda. Closer still, he saw the agent.

A classic herdman, totally forgettable, he stood emptily

by the wall some yards this side of the car. He looked to be waiting with infinite patience for nothing to happen.

Apple halted nearby. He asked aside, "Keys are in the ignition?"

The man said, "Right. Papers in glove compartment. Tank full. Sign on the dotted line."

Apple looked at him, looking for a form. "What?"

"Joke, One," the agent said. "You're not the only clown in the ring." The faint expression in his bland eyes, however, was not of humour but dread.

All operatives, as Apple knew, had a fear of guessing wrong, even if it was about an inconsequence with no espionage connections. The outside small could become the inside big.

Or was it worse in this case?—Apple wondered. Was this man on his way down, and out, because of a series of misguesses, a star reduced to delivery jobs?

Apple hid his chill with a smile, saying, "You're the first person who realized I was joking when I said I used a skylight."

His hairline tightening with relief, the agent turned away and moved off. Apple went to the car, himself feeling relieved.

The Mazda, Apple soon learned, was the sports model, with a roof as low as possible. Anyone under six feet four would be reasonably accommodated. Spine bowed, head down to the peer-over-specs angle, Apple knew that he had met Angus Watkin's revenge for an impertinence.

He drove out of Bloomsbury, heading east. During his thirty-minute crawl in rush-hour traffic he made no mental comment in respect of direction; and when he was driving into Hackney he put on an act of surprise; and when he turned into the street of the storage garage he laughed at the coincidence of being here again so soon. He had only been driving around idly to get the feel of the car.

Apple drew into the side and stopped. He decided that as it was too early for the house, and since he happened to be on the spot, he might as well see if he could locate that old cab.

This time when Apple went through the swing doors, he didn't go up the steps; he went down a flight at their side, one marked above STAFF ONLY. It led him to the garage proper, which had a smell like the singed hems of Arabs' robes.

Apple was right at the edge of the heap of vehicles. There being no signs of life, he entered the maze. Sometimes he could walk, sometimes he had to sidle or squeeze; sometimes he was able to see all around over roofs, sometimes he was being towered over by trucks and buses; sometimes he stopped feeling anxious, and sometimes he felt excited.

He sidled up to a familiar black shape. It was a London taxi. But he saw at once that it was too young to be Ethel. Also, it had rust spots, whereas Ethel had been well taken care of over the years, apart from her dissolute days with the Vice Squad.

Apple went on through the cars. He wondered, with a hope that had a tinge of regret, if there could be no truth to the story of Ethel's dismissal. It was, after all, a hard story. Could be she wasn't going to be sold.

Apple rounded a bus—and stopped. His heart gave one loud, deep thud. He took a short step backwards and part-raised his arms in recognition and greeting, respect and pleasure.

Physically, Ethel looked fine. Those long-time dents were signs of character, best let be: in any case, she was too old to have to suffer the panel-beater's hammer. With new footwear and a tune-up, she would be as good as middle-aged.

Ethel, however, had an air of dejection, Apple noted on

moving forward. One tyre was soft, her paint was dull, her glasswork lacked spirit, her chrome had no glint. She looked forlorn, alone and unwanted, an outcast among a crush of uncouth strangers.

Swallowing, Apple ran a hand along Ethel's body as he went to the front. There, to be on the safe side, he looked for and found the two sets of initials. Patting the radiator he murmured, "All right." Next he moved to the driver's door. He intended to get in, sit at the wheel, feel all that marvellous headroom, fondle the instruments.

Holding the handle, Apple paused. He was savouring the coming intimacy. That was rudely ended by a shout.

Apple swung his head. Approaching through the maze was a squat, bald figure: the man from the office. Behind him came a uniformed guard. The shout was still echoing around the garage.

Apple realized that he must have been seen from the windows above, given away by his traitorous height. He slipped away from Ethel. His speed quickened at another shout, though it was less worry of an involvement than the thought of Angus Watkin finding out about this extramural activity.

Apple skipped, sidled at speed, ran. He twisted and angled along the lanes between vehicles. In a weird sort of way, he was enjoying himself. He even grinned when yet another shout from behind was obviously directed at other guards, who must be somewhere ahead of him.

Apple went at a crouch. He turned a corner, came to a van. Its rear doors were brokenly open. Stopping, Apple hesitated only a moment before eeling through the gap, which he reduced to a slit after turning on hands and knees inside the van's body. He waited. Half the grin was still there.

The bald man came pantingly past. He was followed at a

stride by the security guard, whose eyes were as narrow in grimness as his mouth was agape with fervour.

When the sounds of passage had faded, Apple eased out of the van. One eyebrow was raised in amused tolerance—until a voice behind him said:

"I thought you might be in there."

Apple swung around. The voice belonged to the guard. He was coming forward with reaching hands, still narrow-eyed and gape-mouthed.

Always do the unexpected, ran the adage that was taught in Training Three. Therefore Apple, smiling, went toward the guard instead of the other way. He didn't start on the shove until the very last second. The man fell into a backward stagger, yelling as he went.

Realizing that he now needed to make better time than the lanes allowed, Apple scrambled up onto the front of a car. Standing, he stepped up onto the roof.

To the centre of the next car's roof was about seven feet. For Apple, with his long legs, it was an easy distance. He leapt. He landed.

The resulting boom, plus its echo, made Apple almost lose his balance. During the regaining of it, he saw that the guard was circling below, and that other figures were coming swiftly through the lanes.

Apple leapt to the next car, then the next, and went on leaping amidst a manic, terrifying, continual booming that echoed around the garage like thundering cannon. Apple felt nervously unreal.

Direction he gauged by taking a fix on the office. His fast glances there showed him a line of interested observers standing at the window.

With two final long-leaping jumps, both of which left dents, Apple reached the edge of the cars. It was where he had started. He let himself down and ran to the door.

One minute later he was inside the red Mazda, starting it up. As he pulled away from the kerb, he saw in his rear-view mirror the guard in the act of slowing from a chasing run. The man shook a fist. His mouth was a grim slit, his eyes were wide with lost fervour.

Nothing had changed in the street of tall oaks, Apple saw. He had brought his car to a stop at the corner. Now it was close to eleven o'clock, time for the coffee ritual at Peace Manor. The past hour Apple had spent on a park bench, in the watery sun, reading the pamphlets that bulged his inside left breast pocket in a way that would have made Angus Watkin droop his eyelids—a normal person's scream of rage.

If questioned by the folk singer or anyone else, Apple would be able to say what the pamphlets were about and even quote some of their noble sentiments. He was able to share same in principle. But, on the whole, he thought it might be more gratifying to be a Mormon.

Patting his pocket, raising his head to butt the roof, Apple drove on. He picked up speed quickly and desecrated the street's silence with a series of horn blasts.

Curving, he came to a racing halt nose-in to the gates. Behind them stood the Hammer with the ski-jump nose, whom Apple had christened Gateman. He glared.

Apple put his head out of the window. Glaring back, he called out in Russian, "Open up there, comrade." He added a phrase he had once heard a KGB-plus use to a KGB-minus, which roughly translated as "Shake the lead out, boy."

His glare gone, but not replaced by any other expression, the Hammer opened first one gate and then the other. He stood aside, face to the front; but his eyes were on Apple every second of the way through.

Apple drove on. His features were still stiff with surprise.

He hadn't expected the ploy to work. It was so old it had a pension.

Apple ignored the thought that no pro would have tried such a chestnut; he welcomed the thought that the pro might therefore never have gained an entry.

The driveway forked before reaching the house. To the right stood parked cars. Apple joined them with his Mazda, which he locked after squeezing out, then unlocked because he realized he may need to leave in a hurry, Gateman obliging.

While Apple stood looking at the house in uncertainty, not sure of the manner of his next move, there sounded a burst of restrained laughter. It came, apparently, from somewhere behind the mansion. Apple went that way.

After rounding a clump of tall bushes, their flowers pink, he came to a greenhouse. It also was between himself and the rear of the house. He opened a door at the end and slipped inside. His nose twitched at the hot, sweet stench of jungle growth.

Apple softly walked a wooden path to the far end, where he cut through to the side. The glass was steamy and dribbly. Picking up a fallen leaf, Apple used it to clear one pane. The makers of the laughter were so close that involuntarily he eased back.

There were thirty-odd people. They were formed into five or six separate groups, though still in one general mass. Some stood, most sat in folding chairs. A table in the middle held everything needed for the coffee ceremony.

Apple picked out the Russian Rural Quartet at once. Three were facing this way, one was in profile. All could have passed for men in their seventies; all were fit-looking and seemed alert; all had ample white hair and drooping white moustaches. There was a distinct difference, however, between the trio and the single.

Sitting together, alone, the three were as solemn as children at an adult party. They weren't speaking. Spines not touching the chair backs, they sat upright with folded arms. The impression they gave was of conserving their joy until the next tragedy came along.

The single was a social animal. He sat comfortably, in a slouch, his legs crossed. With a cup in one hand, a cigarette in the other, he was obviously enjoying himself as he chatted to those who semi-fawned around him.

The those (they were mainly British) Apple heard despite the sweat that was beginning to gather in his ears. He found the atrocious Russian painful to listen to, even though it made him feel clever.

He sagged, tapping his knees together, at the next linguistic outrage.

It came from a matron with flustery hands and a stare. Confusing adjectives and gender, she said to the centre of attraction, "You are such a naughty young girl, Josef."

Everyone laughed, including the one addressed, while the three other members of the Russian Rural Quartet slowly turned on each other looks of profound disgust, like hunger-strikers in a kitchen.

Palming the sweat from his face, Apple thought: Josef, eh? Well, Josef, you are the chosen one. You will serve the purpose very nicely.

More coffee was being served. The trio declined with polite swings of their folded arms. Josef accepted. Enunciating carefully, he began to tell a joke.

The singer had a brown, wrinkled face. His lips were stretched tight over false-looking dentures. Though pale and watery, his eyes were sharp and swift. The tip of his nose and his cheeks formed a level line of protuberant globes, like a pawnbroker sign changed in the name of equality. Josef was a tall gnome of a man.

Gasping at the heat, sweating all over, Apple decided he had seen and done enough. He realized that if he were to make an approach here, it would cancel the effect he wanted to make of an ardent Communist trying to win converts. That would have to be done elsewhere.

Shrewd thinking, Porter, Apple told himself while not acknowledging that he should have told himself yesterday. He moved from the window and made his wet way back along the wooden path.

Departure went without a hitch. No one saw him go to the car or leave in it. Gateman opened the way ahead of time in answer to lordly horn blasts. Apple kept his face turned aside while going through.

Altogether a brilliantly managed foray into enemy territory, he decided.

Like the stares of old folks, Apple was hungry. He had not, he remembered on getting the first pang, had any breakfast, only his wake-up pre-run coffee with two sweet biscuits.

On the outer edges of Central London, in a district that was fighting to stay a lower-middle mess, rather than be an upper-lower slum, Apple parked his Mazda, locked it and set off along the street.

From here it wasn't far to a cafe that was operated by a basketball fan and frequented by many local players of the game. Apple knew all the right places.

In the cafe, enjoying the glances of envy/approval if not the food, Apple stodged through a lunch of meat and two veg, suet pud with custard, a pint of strong tea. While paying, he stood at the counter next to a man who was at least seven feet, two inches tall. Apple left feeling sated.

Heading away from the car, he strolled. He lit a cigarette. It was long finished by the time he came to the corner that he recognized. He went around it and then into an alley. He had nothing to say mentally in the matter.

The literature was still there. Squatting, Apple got most

of it into his arms. That one bundle had to be left he felt as unimportant. He looked away from it while rising.

Humming, he went back to the side street, back to the main road, and along to the ex-butcher shop, which he entered without a hum.

There was no one to be seen, though from the rear came a woman's voice. Its song was of the bliss to be had on a collective. Apple quietly eased his load onto the table, turned and quietly left.

Still making no inner comment, though feeling even better than before, Apple went at a comfortable amble back the way he had come.

He started considering various methods, wildest first, of getting into the theatre where the Russian Rural Quartet would be appearing this evening. There would be no hope of buying a ticket for the week's biggest hit.

Presently, Apple stopped thinking doorman-assault on getting the feeling that he was being watched. It wasn't the trailing finger; he had no such sensation across his shoulders. It was an awareness more of company than attention.

When the feeling persisted, proving that it wasn't caused by someone stationary, the idle observer, Apple reasoned that he was being followed in quotes by somebody who was moving ahead of him. This was standard practice, though used more often with car-tailing than on foot.

Cars in mind, Apple ruled out a watcher in a vehicle: the noon traffic was moving too fast.

He started to take notice of the walkers on the street's other side, the side that made back-checking easiest, a half-turn as opposed to a full.

Apple saw his man at once. He was dressed plainly and dimly, but apart from that he was no herdman. He had a dark, saturnine face; he stood out by the fact of wearing a hat; his walk had a jauntiness, while his tallness and thinness were further, minor pointers. Every ten or fifteen seconds he glanced behind.

Although Apple didn't rule out an espionage agent, he put his money on some other field of operations. What, he didn't know, except that no Watkin people were involved. He was still puzzling it over when he realized the oddity of his feeling being fairly constant.

How could that be so, he wondered, when the thin man looked back only at intervals, short though they were?

A twin-job, Apple concluded at once. Cheerfully intrigued, he gave his attention to the people ahead on his own side of the street. All he did was wait for a back-turned face.

When it came, it was under a hat and above a dim suit and it owned a dark complexion. Resemblance, however, ended there. The partner on this side was fat enough to let it show in his rolling gait.

As the man looked front again, Apple flicked his gaze across the street and was in time to see the other man glance around. The fore-tailers were spelling each other beautifully; a first-class team.

For that, and for their contrasting builds, and for their darkness, Apple gave them thc names by which Laurel and Hardy are known in the Spanish-speaking world: Flaco and Gordo. As well as appropriate, it removed the suggestion of menace which had come with their slickness.

Apple decided to take the duo for a nice long walk. Flaco looked as though he would soon run out of energy, Gordo out of breath. They might even give up or give away whatever it was their game happened to be.

Apple continued to gnaw that puzzle, using the Communist Party office as the link, as he strolled on towards where he had left his car.

When he drew closer to it, he noted that both men were

taking shorter breaks between glances; and, on his coming abreast of the Mazda, that they looked back at the same time. But he told himself he could be wrong as to reason. He kept going.

Over the following hour, keeping fat Gordo in the sun, Apple walked at a steady pace. He tried no tricks, did nothing to imply that he had tumbled to the shadowing, and was successful in making himself not be sympathetic. But he learned nothing.

Again sated, Apple allowed one final look behind from each of the dark, now-plaintive faces, before making an abrupt turn and starting to walk back. Himself, he didn't bother to check behind. He did, however, have a casual glance at his watch to give form to his action.

Gradually, Apple quickened his step. In time he was going at a smart clip, each stride as long as he could make it without strain.

After turning off the main road, he waited until he was sure the duo would be in view before breaking into a jog. Half a mile of that, and he speeded up into a loping run.

When finally Apple did look back, doing so neatly, on a corner, Flaco and Gordo were only just visible in the distance, running like old men up a hill. Apple went on—at full speed. He denied to himself that it was the *coup de grâce*.

Circling, he made his way to the car. His shadows had long since been left with nothing to dog but one another. He was intrigued to see, tucked under a window-wiper on the Mazda, a fold of paper. Claiming it nonchalantly, he was disappointed to find himself reading a promotion hand-out about the opening of a new disco.

Half an hour later, Apple got another disappointment.

In the hall of his apartment, lying supine on the floor, he was fighting for his life against a raging jungle beast when he noticed the envelope in a corner. It had patently been slipped under the door.

Pushing Monico off, Apple sat up. He got the envelope and thumbed it open. Inside was a ticket for this evening's performance of folk singers, among whom would be the Russian Rural Quartet.

Now Apple wouldn't be able to use any of the adroit gimmicks he had been working on to get into the Regal Theatre.

He shrugged, rose and thrust aside the thought that he wanted to make the most of a caper which he knew to be hopeless. He went to shower and put on his robe.

A: Individuals with a personal beef who had mistaken him for the object of their intentions.

B: Local detectives who were curious about a well-dressed stranger in their scruffy division.

C: Members of any of a dozen anti-Communist organizations who wanted to know how he fitted into the scene.

D: Lunatics.

On the whole, Apple preferred C, though for D he had a certain fondness. But he wasn't overly impressed with the affair in respect of importance; had, in fact, put it out of his mind by the time he sat down beside the telephone.

The girl who answered had a bright, chirpy voice, as if she was selling something, not working in a government office. She identified herself as Information.

"I'm calling on behalf of a friend," Apple said, craftily. "I wonder if you could tell me, please, how she would go about buying one of the second-hand vehicles that you have there in the garage."

"A private item, sir, or commercial?"

"A bit of each, actually. I mean, it's not a truck or anything. But a car she has her eye on, I think it's one that's been used for hire."

In a confidential tone, Information said, "Well, she couldn't ply for hire with it again. The licence dies when they go through here."

"No, she wants it for herself."

"Okay. So you tell her to attend the auction tomorrow morning in Clapton, starting at ten. That's when they'll polish off all the smaller items."

"Oh, an auction," Apple said. "I suppose there'll be a lot of competition."

"Not much. Mostly car dealers and a few scrap merchants. The older items get bought to be broken up for spare parts and junk metal."

Apple glared ahead sightlessly, chilled. He whispered, "Christ."

"Beg pardon, sir?"

Just thinking aloud, he told her. He rang off after getting the auction mart address.

Apple lit a cigarette. Billowing smoke, he paced back and forth across the living-room. Now there was no question about it, he mused like a furious but muttered argument. Ethel had to be bought. To miss out on getting her, losing her to some young hot-rodder, that would be painful. To have her go to oblivion, that would be agony. It must not happen.

"Never," Apple told Monico, who first raised his head from his crossed legs, next opened his eyes.

Breaking off-course, Apple strode to the writing desk, where he fumbled among papers until he found his chequebook. The most recent stub showed a paltry sum.

"It doesn't matter about the ready cash," Apple assured his dog as he straightened and turned. "There's lots of things here that can be sold or pawned. Dozens. No problem about that. The money is raisable."

Wearing a cruel smile, Apple began to wander around the apartment. His left hand was formed into a fist except for the thumb, which stuck out; it represented the grandfather clock. His index finger was twitchingly ready to poke, waiting to represent the next cashable article.

Apple still looked like a hitch-hiker when he went into the hall. There, he saw the theatre ticket, where he had left it on a slim table. The slip of paper gave him pause. His hand uncurled and his face sagged.

Apple was realizing that he would be expected to make a try at abduction this evening. Angus Watkin, naturally, would have at least one observer on the scene. If agent One did nothing, agent One could very well find himself pulled out, and subsequently sent farther down the ladder than before. In the unlikely event of him ever being used again, outside the language connection, it would be as agent Three-eighty-two.

Apple hurried to the kitchen to plug in the toaster.

"I do hope everything goes smoothly," Ogden Renfrew said in his beautifully modulated voice.

Apple changed gear. "I'm sure it will, Og."

"But there's no need, you know, for the fee. I'd be more than happy to do this for nothing."

"Let's not start that again. You're a pro, and pros must be paid. That's an unwritten law."

Ogden Renfrew shrugged cheerfully. He was a wiry man in the late sixties, with white hair and a gauntly handsome face. Like many of Apple's acquaintances, he was a stranger to success. During forty years as an actor, he had worked only sporadically, and had been "resting" ever since Apple had known him. His main income came from being a voice, dubbing foreign films in English.

He said, "Love works in mysterious ways, its blunders to perform." It was a line from a play in which he had once nearly had a part.

"Love makes the world go round," Apple said. It wasn't very good, but he had a lot on his mind at the moment.

Apple had been busy over the past hours. First he had contacted Ogden Renfrew, to make sure that he was available and to put him on standby. Next he had gone to the Regal Theatre, on Old Compton Street, where he had scouted out the scene. Third he had bought a bowl-crown cap in the East End. Next, from a public telephone, he had called in.

Crisply Apple had requested a car and two operatives, it and they to be at a named place at a stated time. Watkin's response had been a weary-sounding, "Very well, Porter." Last, Apple had called Ogden Renfrew back to finalize arrangements and explain the situation.

Now he needed to go over the latter again, for Renfrew said, "I still can't see how this is going to help."

"The girl-friend, Og. Her name's Anna. She won't believe me that I've finished with Mavis, and I can't persuade Mavis to talk to her, hardly even to me, because she's angry over that thing with Judy. See?"

"No. But never mind that part of it."

"You, Og, are going to play Mavis's father," Apple said, speeding up the Mazda to cross a junction. "You will be coming with me, albeit reluctantly, to where Anna will be waiting in her Rolls-Royce. When nearly there, you'll have a change of heart and hurry back. In fact, you'd better run to make it more convincing. Okay?"

"Okay," the actor said. "Did you say a Rolls?"

"Yes. Or it might be a Jag. So I'll go on and tell Anna that, obviously, you don't want to get in your daughter's bad books, knowing, as you do, that Mavis thinks the world of me. It's pretty good, eh? What d'you think?"

"I think you're out of your mind."

Apple was turning into Old Compton Street. He asked, "Why?"

Ogden Renfrew said, "I suppose you believe that it will increase Anna's ardour if she thinks that there's another woman crazy for you."

"It did when I told her about Judy."

"Someone's insane. Maybe it's me. In my day we used to operate differently, let me tell you." He did, as Apple parked and while they walked along the street together, towards the Regal Theatre, where people were filtering inside. He broke off when Apple led him into an alley.

"What are we doing here?"

"This goes right through to the other street," Apple said. "That's where she'll be waiting later. I want you to meet me right here two hours from now."

"I'll go to the movies," Ogden Renfrew said. "Look, there's the stage door."

"Really?" Apple said in a disinterested tone.

"Passed through it often."

"Well, Og, that's all for now. Any questions?"

"Only one. Why don't you go back to Mavis?" He turned away with a Shakespeare wave. "Fare thee well."

Over the following two hours, Apple wouldn't have minded being at the movies himself. It wasn't that he disliked folk music. It was that he felt he might have had a better chance of losing himself and his worries with a picture, in the dark, away from the onstage bustle and regular bursts of clapping. Nor could he go to the bar at intermission for a much-needed drink; he didn't want to leave his seat, make himself conspicuous.

The Russian Rural Quartet, as though they were top of the bill in a music hall, appeared at the end of the programme. Wearing peasant-style dress, they sang eight songs. Each was slightly worse than the one before; and each earned rapturous applause. Apple had to admit that, taking account of their ages, the four men were probably remarkably average.

He slipped out of his seat while the audience was offering a standing ovation, which, as is customary in Russia, the singers were returning with their own applause.

Outside the theatre, scattered, stood a score of loiterers. Apple recognized that curious breed which likes to feed on the faces of people who are leaving places of entertainment.

He went to and along the alley. There, twice as many people were gathered near the stage door. These had purpose, manifested by their cameras, Russian flags, autograph books and fulsome smiles.

Apple found Ogden Renfrew on the group's periphery. He walked him on and said, "Cap."

From a pocket of his dark suit the actor brought out the bowl-crown cap which Apple had given him earlier. He put it on and snuggled the peak low over his eyes.

Apple said, "Moustache."

Ogden Renfrew produced an item from his own professional tool-box. With a flourish, he stuck the droopy white moustache to his top lip. Now, aided by the meagre lighting, he did bear a fair resemblance to the folk singers.

Apple took hold of his left arm. He moved slightly to his rear as they came out into the street. For the tenth time, Apple assured himself that there was no way Angus Watkin could find out that a genuine snatch attempt had not been made.

Apple saw the Upstairs car. It was a hundred yards away, on the opposite side. There were two men in the front. They gave the on-alert signal by simultaneously raising lighted cigarettes to their mouths.

"Where is this Anna?" Ogden Renfrew asked. "I don't see any Rollses. Nor Jags."

"She might be in the Daimler tonight. She has a car for every day of the week."

"Christ," the actor said in a voice that was void of beauty and modulation. "Forget Mavis."

They were almost midway to the car. Far enough, Apple decided. He said, "Okay, Og, pull away now and take off. I'll fall down to make more of a production out of it. A bit of theatre never hurts."

"Good lad," Ogden Renfrew said. "And goodbye." He ripped his arm free of Apple's hold and swung himself away like an outraged Hamlet.

Apple fell. He landed on his hands, rolled over onto his back. With satisfaction he listened to the sound of the actor's rapid footfalls; with dismay, he heard a car door crash open and a starter begin to yammer.

Apple raised his head, took a fast look around. A man was coming, running obliquely across the roadway. The car engine started and its lights came on.

Apple switched the other way. Ogden Renfrew, trotting elegantly, had still not reached the alley's mouth.

Feeling frozen with shock, unable to rise, Apple again shifted his view. The running agent was almost here, on the pavement, while the car was squealing away from the kerb. In respect of the first, Apple thought, there was only one thing to be done.

The agent, running full out, threw himself up into a leap to clear Apple, who was lying across the pavement, and who quickly imitated the act of awkward rising by kicking his legs in the air. One leg got lucky.

Tripped, the agent went into headlong flight. To Apple's relief, he landed expertly and took himself on into a roll. With more relief Apple saw beyond the rolling form that Ogden Renfrew had gone from sight.

The car was coming to a stop nearby as Apple and the operative started to get up. But only Apple went all the way to full upright. The agent stayed in a crouch. He was staring at something on the ground in front of him.

Stepping closer, Apple saw that the object of interest was a white moustache.

"Ruined," he moaned. "Destroyed." He was striding out a well-known path in the living-room at Harlequin Mansions. His arms he swung sideways instead of straight. He was so distraught that he hadn't thought to put on his robe. "Knackered. Screwed. Totally ballsed up." He would have used stronger language had he been alone, though all that could be seen of Monico was a tail sticking out from behind the armchair.

"Unless I can come up with a brilliant cover story," Apple said. "And right now. Before bloody Watkin calls. Which he's bound to. Any minute. Believe me. No, no, there's no time for toast. The call's going to come at any second." He looked at the telephone.

It rang.

Apple stopped pacing with a jerk. After a pause he went into a money-lender stoop over clasped hands to walk at a measured step over to the telephone table. He lifted the receiver between finger and thumb.

The caller was Professor Warden. He enquired solicitously after the blood pressure. Apple, in a fumble, told him and thanked him and rang off as soon as he could.

Before Apple could move away, the telephone shrilled again. He picked up the handset wearily and heard a gasped, "I've lost my tash somewhere. I'm very upset. I've had it for years. I understudied Lear in that tash. It's real sable. What'm I going to do?"

Apple assured Ogden Renfrew that his moustache was safe and undamaged, promised to deliver it soonest, disconnected.

Pacing again, after having dismissed the ploy of leaving the receiver off its cradle, it occurred to Apple that he could say that the Russian Rural Quartet were phonies.

They were really only eighty years old. They wore white wigs and false moustaches.

Swinging his arms sideways, Apple said, "No good. Every face-losing country in the West's checked them out. They're genuine. It could've worked, though, if not for that. I didn't give anything away, you know. I was cool."

In the street, with one agent still staring down and the other on hold half-way out of the car, Apple had stooped to retrieve the V of white hairs. Slipping it into his pocket, he had said a croaky:

"Thank you. That's all. Good night." He had walked on in a daze of defeat.

The telephone rang.

Apple detoured to it as if climbing the thirteen steps. He lifted the receiver with both hands and bent his head to meet it tenderly. At hearing Angus Watkin's voice he smiled sadly. He said:

"I was just about to call in, sir. I got back here two minutes ago."

"And for my part," Watkin drawled, "I have just finished speaking with agents Two and Three."

"Oh," Apple said. "Yes."

"I'm on scrambler at this end, Porter. A new gadget. It makes you sound totally different."

"Really, sir?"

"You could even be someone else. Which would be quite amusing. Please describe the tie I was wearing the last time we met."

Apple did so. And in the act, he found the answer. Later, thinking about it, he would come to the conclusion that it was mentioning the herringbone weave in the tie material that had brought a red herring to his mind; at the moment, he thought of nothing but his luck and/or brilliance.

From the description he blundered straight on into,

"You'll have guessed, sir, of course, what happened this evening. Though I don't know if Two and Three tumbled. Naturally I didn't go into the matter with them."

Weak with release, Apple while speaking had let himself sag in every muscle. He ended up sitting cross-legged on the floor. At about the same time, Monico, coming out of hiding, jumped up onto the chair.

Angus Watkin was giving nothing away. Greedily he said, "Tell me how you see it, Porter."

"It was someone else, sir. And I'm pleased to say that I had my suspicions from the beginning. It was just a shade too easy, the way he came out of the stage door alone. But I couldn't afford to miss the opportunity. I know you'll agree with that. So I took his arm in grip forty and marched him along the alley."

"Spare me the blow-by-blow account, Porter. You are not a police constable giving evidence in court."

"No, sir," Apple said, holding the receiver airily in one hand. "I didn't tumble until out on the street, when I spoke to him in Russian. He answered in perfect English. I let go at once, of course, and he ran off—after knocking me down. So that was the set-up, sir. They were using a decoy, as I had suspected."

Watkin said, "Mmm."

"The false moustache makes that absolute. It wasn't simply someone who happens to resemble the singers that I grabbed."

Again Watkin said, "Mmm."

"And I might've fallen for it, and taken him to the safe-house, thereby giving away its location, if it hadn't been for my knowledge of Russian. I'm beginning to see, sir, why I was chosen for this operation."

The humming sound made this time by Angus Watkin lasted longer. As it was coming to an end, Apple saw how he could get additional aid for himself out of the story. He said:

"Therefore it would appear, sir, since it's obvious that the KGB expect trouble, that this is not going to be an easy operation. I was able to outwit them this time, but the future looks shaky. I have severe doubts about being able to bring this caper off."

After a short silence, Angus Watkin said, "You mustn't jump to conclusions, Porter. A decoy the man certainly could have been. He could also have been an innocent nobody, one who was wearing a false moustache for some joke or serious reason of his own."

"That *is* a possibility, sir," Apple said. He was quite happy to cancel additional aid so long as the fiasco was smoothed over.

"You might bear that in mind tomorrow."

"Yes, sir. Tomorrow?"

Angus Watkin said, "I have in my possession the Soviet visitors' social schedule. Because of the folk singers' popularity, it isn't being made public. They would be swamped by well-wishers and generally inconvenienced."

"And tomorrow, sir?"

"At eleven o'clock in the morning they will be going on a sightseeing trip to the Monument. You know where that is, I trust."

You rotten old bastard, Apple thought happily. He was pleased with the place. A famous landmark always replete with tourists, it would be ideal for the presenting of himself as a Communist proselytizer.

"I do, sir, yes," Apple said. "It was designed by Sir Christopher Wren to commemorate the Great Fire. It has three hundred and eleven steps inside of black marble. There's a marvellous view from the top."

"Porter—"

"As a matter of fact, the height of the column, which is fluted, is two hundred and two feet, and that is the exact distance from the column's base to the house in Pudding Lane where the fire broke out."

"Porter," Angus Watkin said, his voice coming close to betraying a shade of emotion. "I merely enquired of you if you were familiar with location."

"Sorry, sir."

Another brief silence followed before Angus Watkin continued, with, "The Russian Rural Quartet are getting the very maximum in casual exposure, which is intended to show how unfettered Soviet nationals are. They will circulate freely."

"That's good news, sir."

"There will, however, be guards present, if only to afford protection from molesters and maniacs."

"That's understandable, sir," Apple said. "And possibly there'll be more decoys."

As if he were deaf, Angus Watkin said, "But the guards will be discreet. You will not see them, Porter."

While fluent in several languages, Apple was also expert in Watkinese. The foregoing he translated as, "A pro would spot the guards easily, but an amateur like yourself . . ."

Apple said a suave, "I shall do my best, sir."

Angus Watkin sighed. He said, "Good night, Porter."

CHAPTER 3

The car auction was held in a long, narrow shed. It looked as though it had once been a cover for a train. Top and sides were of corrugated iron, windows were glassless gaps. Every local breath of wind came to help prove the tunnel principal, making for a steady breeze.

Sole piece of furniture was a table. Standing on it were the auctioneer and his clerk, each with one shoulder raised against the wind. Less affected were the sixty to seventy men who stood below, on either side of a paint-indicated lane.

Apple's hair was flopping and twirling like a mob of speedy drunks. At first he had settled it occasionally with his hand. Because of that he had nearly bought a Dodge convertible with decent rubber, a new transmission and yellow seat-covers. He had needed to make urgent signs to let the auctioneer know that he wasn't bidding. Now he allowed his hair to cavort freely, despite this adding appreciably to his height.

The vehicles, each bearing a numbered card, stretched away in single file along the shed and outside. Two nonchalant youths were the drivers. As one took a knocked-down car on, out of the crowd, the other brought the next one in on the painted lane.

A motor auction being for him a new experience, Apple was intrigued. He made mental note of everything: the expression of glaring integrity on the auctioneer's face, and the poetry he employed to describe each car; the clerk's panning looks of disgust when bids were slow in coming; the dealers' secret methods of bidding, from winks to nose-picks, and their open derision for the poet.

Ethel was number eighteen. Number thirteen had just been driven in. Since trade was brisk, Apple reckoned he would be getting down to business in about twenty minutes.

Happily he began to debate what bidding method he should use. Himself, he rather fancied a slow, graceful nod.

"This little gem," the auctioneer said, his hoarse voice throbbing, "is not only a pleasure to gaze upon, it is also a joy to drive. Inside that graceful body beats a healthy and noble heart."

Nodding encouragement while ignoring the coarse sniggers, Apple looked over heads at the ancient Rover. It was blue where not embossed with a delicate filigree of rust, cracked where unenhanced by sculpted dents, shiny where missed by the cloudy patina of age.

After more praise, the auctioneer asked, "Who'll start me off with four hundred pounds?"

From all around conversation began. It seemed to be mostly about dog-racing and the price of beer. Above the jabber a voice rose, calling, "Fifty quid."

Apple looked around in order to identify the rash bidder and saw Flaco.

The thin, dark man was entering by a door close to the back of the crowd. He wore his hat at a determined angle. His eyes were busy.

Apple, in the sliver of time, dropped from sight. This he did with a well-practiced sag at the knees. A man at his side glanced at him with a suspicious frown, another to his rear said, "Thanks, mate."

Apple sidled away. In a different location he risked a quick bob up. Flaco had started to circulate through the crowd. There was no sign of Gordo.

Which was something, Apple thought fretfully. It might be possible to keep ahead of Flaco, with luck; and, with flashes of brilliance, still make bids for Ethel. If she came on the block soon.

With his clerk sneering, the auctioneer was pleading for a better opener on the Rover. Several men left beer and dogs long enough to shout, "Take it away." Apple willed for them to be obeyed.

He moved on again after a bob up, which showed him the slow but steady approach of Flaco. From that, Apple got an idea. He went farther on and spent five minutes gradually, unobtrusively making three quarters of a circle. Now he had Flaco ahead of him. He kept him there, trailing three yards back. His thighs ached.

After being knocked down for fifty pounds, the Rover had been replaced by a newish MG. Bidding was fast. The auctioneer soon reached the handclap that followed his going-going-gone. The next car, also newish, also a Customs and Excise confiscation, also went quickly.

Apple was cheering up—until a decrepit Singer came creaking in. He snatched a look at his watch. With a surprise that caused him to straighten to his full height plus wind-whipped hair, he saw that the time was twenty minutes to eleven. And it would take him at least ten minutes to reach the Monument.

Flaco was turning around. Apple shot down. He chewed his bottom lip and felt hate for the auctioneer, who was declaiming an ode to the Singer's perfection.

The crowd eddied. Apple knew it meant that Flaco was making a reverse tour. He turned and went the other way. If this didn't stop soon, he thought, his thigh muscles were going to burst. He joined others in shouting, "Take it out."

It occurred to Apple that he could buy the car himself to hurry matters along. But that might leave him short for Ethel, and he might be too short already.

It was a quarter to eleven. Apple gasped with relief when a man's called offer of thirty pounds was snapped up in a handclap. The Singer creaked out.

Fearing that he could have been mistaken and might come face to face with Flaco, Apple risked a bob. He couldn't locate the thin man. It took two more up-jerks before he saw him. He was walking away along the line of waiting cars.

Apple stayed at full stretch to rest his thighs. He prayed for Flaco to keep going, hoped for someone to make a bid on the wreck in the middle, willed time to go slowly.

But the thin man turned back midway, the auctioneer went on pleading, and now it was ten minutes to eleven. Apple had to go. He had to put career before private life. He had to leave Ethel to her fate.

Hurting inside, back in his sag, Apple began to reverse through the crowd. The door being dangerously far, he edged towards a window. He made it unseen and slipped through the gap. One racing minute later, he was within sight of his red car—and Gordo.

The fattish man, like any rank amateur (or playing at one?—Apple wondered) was pretending to read a newspaper. He stood on the kerb two cars along from the Mazda. Amid the bustle of foot and wheeled traffic, his concentration to the experienced was as likely as a stripper playing La Scala.

Apple had slowed to a striding walk. He kept going. With a jaunty whistle and a far-pitched gaze, he went straight past Gordo, who had raised his newspaper higher.

Apple didn't look back, nor try for the mirror-view in shop windows. He strode on until coming to a small Woolworth's, towards which he angled smartly, the while glancing at the upper floor, as if that were his destination.

Inside, Apple hastened along to another door and stood within its frame. When via a peek he saw Gordo come in the store, he slipped outside and ran back to the car. He would have thought how clever he was except for thinking about Ethel.

Apple estimated that there were some three hundred people around the Monument, milling, gaping, lounging, snapshotting. Most were tourists, from home and abroad; and many were of the non-culture clan, Apple realized, which accounted for the celebrated folk singers going largely unnoticed.

The four old men, separated into trio and single, were a part of the crowd. They stood talking casually with other people—a mainly British entourage, Apple guessed. But that was the only guess he was inclined to hazard in respect of the Russians.

Angus Watkin had been right, Apple found to his quiet fury. He was unable to spot one person, male or female, who could conceivably be a KGB watchdog. There were no high Hammer shoulders, no thick Sickle waists, none of the other tell-tale signs blatant or subtle.

Circulating, drawing closer to the Soviets, Apple told himself that a whole new breed of operatives could have been fielded by Moscow in recent times. He wouldn't know. He was only a faceless one.

Cheer up there, One, Apple thought. Stiffen that upper lip. Get that shoulder to . . .

He was being stared at.

Apple did a slow, planned double take. It lasted merely one second, during which he pinpointed the starer and recognized him as ski-nosed Gateman, as well as interpreting his stare as one that asked its producer a question: where have I seen that man before?

Going into a semi-sag, Apple moved behind a knot of people. He felt sure that Gateman would not be able to answer the question and soon put it out of mind. For himself, he supposed he must have missed spotting the Hammer first time round, which could be the same with others.

But Apple still hadn't seen any by the time he was edging ever closer to where Josef, smiling, was signing autographs for a pair of Boy Scouts. Ten feet away, the three other old singers were also signing books, though solemnly.

Apple drew pamphlets from his pocket. He plunged as soon as the Scouts turned away, beating another autograph hunter. He stopped close beside Josef and pressed a pamphlet into his hand.

In English, Apple said, "Please read this, sir. You may find it interesting."

Josef smilingly shook his head while saying, in Russian, that he didn't understand, he had no English. Apple performed a gape of surprise and delight. Using the old man's language, but as badly as pride would allow, he said:

"You are from the Soviet Union! How wonderful that I should meet you by accident like this. It is my dream to visit Moscow. I am a member of the British Communist Party and . . ." Apple gushed on. He was glad to see boredom colour the polite smile worn by Josef, who broke in at length to ask what was the pamphlet he had been given. Told, he pushed it back. The three globes of his face, nose and cheeks quivered as his smile fought for life. He said:

"No, thanks, son. There's quite enough of that where I come from. Goodbye." Circling the autograph hunter he moved off at the speed of a stripling.

"Oh," Apple said dully. He stood watching Josef as, slowly now, he began to mingle with the crowd and worked at accepting that his marvellous idea had laid an elaborate egg.

A movement caused Apple to look around. The three other folk singers were coming towards him. Their attitude appeared to be a cross between the wary and the menacing.

Apple flashed on a smile. When it wasn't returned by the trio, he turned and slipped away.

Absently stuffing the pamphlet back in his pocket with the others, Apple went in steady pursuit of the Quartet's fourth member. Although his idea had flopped, he was encouraged by Josef's response.

Checking over heads, Apple noted that the trio had become stationary and that the Hammer with the ski-jump nose was gazing about him amiably.

When Apple got within fuller view of his subject, it was to find him in busy, close-leaning conversation. The other person was a youngish man with a Vandyke. Despite the beard, Apple recognized him instantly as one of the herd, an operative, and wondered how he could have missed him earlier. The severe, foreign cut of his dark suit was enough of a give-away.

Taking Josef's arm, the operative began to talk with more urgency. He pointed. Josef nodded. They started to walk towards the edge of the crowd.

The explosion made Apple cry out.

His cry was one among many. Everyone swung around to face the direction of the noise, at the same time cringing or preparing for flight.

The next noise to fill the area was a burst of laughter. Everyone relaxed, including Apple.

Unlike those near him and behind him, those who were now moving forward to investigate, he had the height to see the street entertainer in clown's whiteface and patchwork clothes. The busker was about to light another giant firecracker.

Although Apple moved forward with the others, he had a distinct sensation of discomfort. He didn't know why. He liked fireworks, liked the entertainment which always followed the attention-grabber.

Apple had almost reached the busker, following another explosion, when the answer came. It was *Diversion.*

Apple whipped around and raced back.

Again his tallness was useful. He saw clearly. There was a grey car with a man at the wheel. The rear door was open. By it stood Josef and the operative. Josef wasn't smiling. He was unable to, Apple knew.

The singer's elbow was being held in grip forty. It paralysed the arm and rendered speech or expression difficult, while allowing the lower body to act normally, follow the gripper's commands.

Apple realized that he had been right about the operative's profession, but wrong in assuming him to be a Hammer. His employing nation wasn't Russia; it was any one of those that were currently suffering a loss of face due to the Quartet's success, and his mission was obviously a duplicate of the one set up by Angus Watkin.

As Apple, still racing, dodged around yet another stroller, the man with the Vandyke pushed Josef roughly into the car. He followed inside. The door closed. The car shot away.

Perfect. Couldn't be better. If these two get away with it, and it looks as if they already have, then agent One is in the clear. He won't have failed, the end object of the operation will have been realized, Watkin could have no cause to complain. All perfect. So why doesn't agent One stop?

Apple was running. He ran in the road. It was busy with two-way traffic, which travelled at a speed to suit the near-noon congestion. Apple had overtaken a bus and two trucks and now was being passed by a drop-head. He waved it on.

The grey abduction car came in and out of view among the traffic far ahead.

Because, Apple told himself in reply, the poor old man

might have no wish for an enforced exile, as already accepted. In spite of being bored with Red dogma, he could still love his homeland, want to be with his family. Also, in respect of this moment, he was probably sitting there terrified.

Apple ran on. He was both cheerful and concerned.

Due to heightened awareness, superrecent events seemed to have covered an extended period. But Apple knew that only about three minutes had passed since the first explosion. The unseeable guards couldn't be far behind. If he got outdistanced himself, they might manage to effect a rescue.

There were traffic lights in the distance. Apple caught a lucky glimpse of the grey car as it turned left, against the red. Apple hoped there was a policeman around the corner.

He changed up to full speed, running the way he had once been coached to do, for a caper in the world of athletics. He passed the drop-head which had overtaken him seconds ago, went on the inside to go by a road-hogging lorry, came to the lights and turned left with his trunk in a lean.

With traffic thinner here, the abduction car was zooming in and out to pass other vehicles. Hopeless, Apple thought, and for the first time considered a chase car. But he could see no taxies, nothing appropriate.

Apple ran on, encouraged by seeing that the snatchers had been stopped, caught behind cars at another set of lights.

A motor cycle shot by like a beast with bad breath. It snarled to a stop in the kerb some way ahead. The driver, in T-shirt and jeans, braced with his feet and gazed around.

Apple headed for him.

The man was young, blond, crew cut and looked as

though he had been born bored. Teeth bared, he was biting off the tail of a yawn as Apple stopped by his side.

"Police," Apple gasped. "Emergency."

The blond clopped his mouth. "That right?"

"Scotland Yard," Apple said. From his breast pocket he took and flashed a card. It proved that bearer was a paid-up member of the Bloomsbury Billiards Club. "I am commandeering this machine, with you as driver. All right?"

"Sure. I like to keep sweet with the pigs."

Apple swung onto the pillion. "Follow that car."

"You know," the blond lazed out, with a rev in between, "that's one of those things I've never had the urge to say."

"Never mind."

"But be that as it may. Which car?"

"I'll show you. Move on, please. The Metropolitan Police will thank you for this."

"Wow," the man said. He took his motor cycle spurtingly away—and the boredom/torpor went out of his manner. He swayed self and machine over to a sickening angle to curve to the crown of the road. Apple grabbed handfuls of T-shirt. He wished he hadn't bothered.

The man shouted back, "You were saying?"

The lights on green, the abductors were speeding ahead and passing cars. Apple said, "That grey Taunus. See? Catch up to it, please."

"Who are they?"

"Anti-noise demonstrators. They've been smashing motor bikes and things like that."

"Bastards," the blond yelled. He missed the front of a bus by inches. "Hanging's too good."

The traffic lights switched to yellow. Apple's right foot pressed downward as though it were on a brake pedal and he wondered what in the world would become of Monico if he got killed. The lights turned to red.

Apple almost fell off the pillion when, close at hand, a screaming started. It was the sound that police sirens used to make before they changed over to the yip-yip. It was coming from the blond.

He sped on towards the junction and its red light. Apple, closing his eyes, waited for disaster.

Poor Ethel, he thought as he was thrown into a lurch one way; poor me as he was jerked the other; poor maniac blond as the screaming rose to a crescendo.

Rose and then chopped off. Apple opened his eyes. The junction had been left behind. The grey car was in clear view, two or three hundred yards ahead, Josef's white hair gleaming in the window.

The man shouted back, "How did that grab you?"

"Fiercely," Apple said. "But now we have to stop those bastards."

"How?"

Apple thought about it while the gap ahead shrank to fifty feet. He said, "I don't know."

The man shook his head. "Don't you ever watch telly? All you have to do is shoot out a tyre."

"I'm not carrying a gun."

"Okay. So what you do is, you punch the driver."

"How can I?" Apple yelled.

"I'll draw alongside and you belt him one."

"He's sure to know about that gimmick. He'll have the window rolled up."

"You're a hard man to please," the blond shouted. He was now right behind the Taunus. "How about standing up and then jumping onto the top of the car?"

"No, thanks," Apple said. He added, as a screaming started again, this time a yip-yip, "I don't think that's going to help us."

"Then what're they doing here?" the man said.

At which point Apple realized that the noise was real; real and coming from behind. A patrol car was in pursuit of the motor cycle for jumping the lights.

Apple glanced back. Roof-light flashing, the police car was swiftly closing in. Apple turned to the blond and yelled, "Pull alongside the bastards."

The machine swooped out, drew level. The driver of the grey car looked around with a snap. He was horse-faced and anxious, like a stallion at the gelding shed.

The window was down. Apple blinked his regret at the no-hope impulse to belt the driver one. But he did manage a good snarl when he spoke.

Not knowing nationality, yet sure that because of this mission Russian would be a necessity, Apple used that language for, "The game's over. Pull in the side and stop." Overriding his words neatly was the siren's insistent yell.

As Apple had expected, the driver started to obey. This was no life-or-death mission. It was more of a show-case caper. For that same reason there would be no violence.

The blond drew ahead and began to slow. When speed had lessened almost to the walking rate, Apple dismounted. He did so simply by standing up on his long legs and letting the cycle go from under him.

The Taunus had stopped. As Apple strode towards it, one hand resting inside his jacket, the police car went wailing past to join the motor cycle.

The driver and the bearded man were sitting still and expressionless, like bad poker players. Josef, behind the driver, showed no signs of fear. He looked intrigued—and as much with Apple as with his companions.

For a brief moment, Apple thought he could have been wrong about the set-up; that the three were all on the same side; that Josef was merely being taken somewhere by part of the Soviet entourage.

But then the driver said, glancing up through the window, "We have diplomatic immunity." His Russian was only fair and it had a German accent.

The man with the Vandyke was more fluent. He said, "You cannot give us a ticket for speeding."

"Good try," Apple said. "But I'm not giving, I'm taking." As the three inside switched away from him to look ahead, he glanced around.

The motor cycle was ten yards on, the police car some yards ahead of that. Two uniformed men were talking to the blond, who, as Apple watched, pointed towards the Taunus.

Josef spoke up. He asked, "Who are you?"

For an answer, Apple opened the rear door. "Get out, please, comrade. You're safe now."

"You must be KGB."

Unseen by the others, Apple nodded. Anything would do for the time being. "Hurry, please," he said, looking back the way they had all come.

Apple expected Soviet guards to appear at any second. There would, he knew without a doubt, be several cars out on the chase/hunt.

Alighting from the Taunus, Josef said, "Well, I hope you can explain all this to me. These two types are as talkative as oysters."

"And just as slippery," Apple said. He checked the other scene ahead. One of the policemen seemed about to come walking this way.

Josef closed the door. Apple told the men inside, speaking German, "On your way, gentlemen, and don't try anything else like this, not on British soil. The pigeons belong to us."

"What're you saying?" Josef asked. It was almost unheard under the sound of the Taunus moving off with a roar like released frustration.

Coughing at exhaust fumes, Apple took the old man's arm and drew him over to the kerb. He said, "I told them to leave you alone."

"But what did they want?"

"They must've said something to you in that respect."

"No. Only that I'd be all right if I kept quiet and behaved myself." He snorted indignantly. "I've never behaved myself in my life."

"Earlier. At the Monument. What was the bearded one talking to you about?"

Josef said, "Told me he sold dirty pictures. Had some in the car if I was interested. What were they really up to?"

"They're reporters from a German magazine," Apple said. "They'll go to any lengths to get a personal interview. Quite ruthless."

Dismissing the matter with a shrug, the folk singer took a step backwards to ease his neck and said, "Regardless of that rotten broken accent you put on back at the Monument, I felt you had to be Russian."

"Did you?"

"They don't grow 'em as tall as you anywhere else."

"Well," Apple said. "Yes." He was thinking furiously to see how he could use the error. He was also watching the traffic behind. He was furthermore keeping a check on the other scene, which hadn't changed.

Josef said, "And, of course, you had to be KGB. I've been approached before with that pamphlet routine. I always enjoy pulling the piss-off-comrade reaction. It gives you people something to think about."

Apple nodded slowly. "In my case," he said, "it was a way of talking to you without the underlings knowing. But you'd gone before I could get started."

"Underlings?"

"I should introduce myself. I'm Colonel Blatski."

Although Josef didn't blanch at the rank, his manner became more deferential. He produced a formal, bowing, "How do you do, colonel."

"Comrade will suffice, comrade. Especially as I'm incognito. Don't mention to anyone that you've met me."

While Josef was saying that he could play the oyster himself if he had to, Apple checked the other scene again. He was sent dreary by seeing that the policeman who had so long been on the point of coming over was now doing just that.

Quickly Apple said, "Can you get away this afternoon? I don't know how tight a clamp the underlings are keeping on you people. That's not my department."

Josef said, "We can go out alone for walks. I don't know if we're watched or not."

"I see."

"I mean guarded in the name of protection."

"Of course you do."

"And I didn't mean what I said when you first spoke to me."

"Of course you didn't."

Josef asked, "Why don't you talk to me now, comrade?"

"That would be difficult," Apple said, turning away. He grandly held up a hand at the approaching policeman and called out in English, "One moment, please, officer."

It might have been surprise, Apple's manner or his height, or belief in the blond's story of his passenger being with Scotland Yard. Whatever, the policeman came to a stop.

"What did you say to him, comrade?"

Apple turned back. "Only that he should mind his own business. These underlings all think they have a right to know what's going on."

Josef looked impressed. "They're KGB?"

"Yes. And I have to get them away from here before some real police show up."

"Naturally. Diplomatic immunity doesn't cover the wearing of official uniforms."

"Quite. Which is why I can't talk to you now. Therefore, comrade, shall we say three o'clock, outside the post office in Muswell Hill?"

"If I can find it."

"A taxi. As soon as you can after leaving Peace Manor, get a taxi. It will take you there, to Muswell Hill. You have English money?"

"Not a single shilling, comrade."

"They don't use shillings anymore," Apple said, digging in a pocket. He tensed on having his watch on the traffic finally rewarded. Coming along behind a bunch of pedal-cyclists was a car whose driver had a ski-jump nose. Beside him sat a man dressed as a priest. In the back seat was a man in the uniform of a bus driver.

Crouching, Apple thrust a five-pound note into Josef's hand. He said, "Some of the underlings are here. That fool who tends to the gate and two others. See them?"

"Yes," the old man said. "Took 'em long enough."

Still in a crouch, Apple began to move away semi-sideways. Hurriedly he said, "Tell them about the reporters. Say they let you go when you refused to speak, except to threaten them with legal action. Say you were trying to make yourself understood to me, a passer-by, so that you could ask for directions. All right?"

"Yes, comrade. Until later, at Muswell Hill."

Apple went on. Head down and shoulders bowed he strode past the waiting policeman without giving him a glance, strode past the other officer and the blond in similar fashion, and went to the police car. He got into it swiftly. Looking at a peep through the rear window, he saw that the KGB car had come to a stop beside Josef, who was standing with folded arms in an about-bloody-time stance.

The two policemen, tailed slouchingly by the blond,

came to the patrol car. The leader leaned inside, touched the peak of his cap and said politely:

"May we see your warrant card, Inspector?"

At the local police station, it took Apple five minutes to get the blond absolved of blame and sent on his bored way, one hour and twenty minutes to win clearance for himself. That time was spent waiting—after he had called in and explained the situation to Angus Watkin.

Finally, to the disappointment of the apprehending pair of officers, the desk sergeant, three detectives and a superintendent, a small bland man entered timidly and gave assurances that the suspect was indeed doing part-time work for Scotland Yard.

Cover unblown, Apple left and went to a nearby pizza palace. He happily ate his way through the family-size sardine and mushroom.

All in all, Apple thought he was doing extremely well. Even Watkin hadn't sounded too totally unperturbed, meaning piqued, at agent One asking him to go through all the necessary channels to avoid a charge of impersonating a police officer.

After lunch, Apple took a taxi back to the mews where he had left his red Mazda. He drove off with a professional flourish and pretended to be unaware of his fish-flavoured burps. Also, briefly, he pretended that Anastasia lounged at his side, her skirt riding high on silk-clad thighs.

Fifteen minutes later Apple walked into the auction mart. The long shed was deserted. There were neither people nor vehicles. Cigarette butts rolled around in the breeze like hardy snowflakes.

Snooping outside, Apple found a chicken hut on wheels. It had a window like a theatre box-office, which, in answer to a tap, opened with a squeak that made Apple's teeth dither.

The man had a shrivelled, pale-blue face. He was dressed for winter in coat, scarf, mittens and a cap with ear-flaps. One of the last he lifted, his head turned sideways, to listen to Apple's enquiry.

Staying in the same pose, the man said, "Top secret, mate. Real hush-hush. Our customers, see, they don't want no one to know nothing."

"But I dare say, sir, that you could give me the name of number eighteen's purchaser, if you felt like it."

"I dare say. If I felt like it."

Apple said, "I'll give you a pound."

Although he kept his face turned away, the man dropped the ear-flap. He said, "I didn't hear that."

"I said I'll give you two pounds."

The flap went up. "I heard that."

Apple put money on the shelf. The man took it, checked a book, said a frontal, "Grinning Jim Jolly. Car dealer. Down near the Elephant."

"Thank you. Most obliging."

"Me, I'm fond of a bit of the old bribery."

"That's nice."

The man said, "I mean, there's not a lot of it about nowadays, is there?

"Money," Apple said, "is the world's most accomplished linguist."

The man winked and closed the window.

Licking his teeth, Apple left. He went to the Mazda feeling smooth and cynical, the seasoned pro. This mission, he mused, was developing very well.

Apple had no trouble in quashing the niggle which said that succeeding here had nothing whatever to do with the mission. He even wondered in passing if he should put the two pounds on his expense account.

The lot belonging to Grinning Jim Jolly stretched back

vastly from a main road in the Elephant and Castle. It was like a dead traffic jam on an eight-lane highway.

Apple walked a path between cars, heading for a slick building at the rear of the pack. One vehicle brought him to a shuddery stop.

It had seen younger and better days as a taxi. Now all that remained of the original was the front. The back had gone, replaced by a pick-up body.

Chased by the thought of men somewhere at this minute hacking cruelly at Ethel's torso, Apple hurried on. He reached the building, climbed steps to a verandah, went into an expansive office.

Everything gleamed. Even the flowers were shiny. Light flashed on the make-up of the girl who sat at a sterile desk. Looking up from polishing a nail-file, she asked:

"Yes, darling?"

Apple said, "I'd like to see Mr. Jolly, please."

"Sorry, darling. Our Jim's out on one of those long liquid lunches. You know. But maybe I can help you."

Apple explained about the auction and about having to leave before eighteen came on the block because his mother was sick. He ended worriedly, "The thing is, I was born in that taxi. I've just got to have it."

The girl added to her shine by blinking moistly. She said, "I think that's terribly sweet, sir."

"Perhaps I'm too sentimental."

"Not at all. I wish Mr. Jolly was here."

"When will he be back?"

"God knows," the girl said hopelessly. "He might not show up for days."

They sighed at each other. Apple produced cigarettes. He forgave himself for the lies because they were in a good cause: the prevention of vandalism.

Lighting the cigarette that the secretary had accepted from him, he asked, "What do you suggest?"

She blew smoke up in the air, leaned down under it and said, "If I were you, what I'd do is this. Leave an offer, plus a cheque for ten per cent of that amount, so he'll know that you're serious."

"Fine," Apple said. "But I've no idea what kind of an offer to make. What's the usual?"

"Can't help you there, sir, I'm afraid. I don't know a thing about car values. I'm just a pretty face. At any rate, Mr. Jolly says I am."

"He's an excellent judge. You're very pretty indeed." This, at least, was true, Apple thought. Her prettiness managed to show through the cosmetics.

The girl nodded. "It is true, I guess. But it's not like being born in a taxi. That's something you'll have all your life." She nodded again. "Take my word for it."

"Yes. And, as you know, one turns more to one's roots the older one gets."

Stubbing her cigarette, the girl got up. She gave him an old-fashioned look and said, "Excuse me, sir. Be back in a minute."

Apple lifted his eyebrows in conjecture. After the girl had left the room, he turned and stepped over to the wide window. The cars stretched away to the road, with dotted about on the paths a few browsers. One man was looking with interest at the taxi-truck.

Lighting a new cigarette from the stub of the old one, Apple began to pace. Patience, One, he warned himself. The girl would be back before you could say Jack Vandal—Robinson. She had to go to the loo or ask someone's advice or see if she could contact Grinning Jim.

Apple went on pacing. He lit another cigarette, smoked it down to the filter, squashed it out with a face of disgust for the fug in his mouth. If he hadn't known he was a liar, he would have sworn never to smoke again.

Back at the window, Apple was feeling in a pocket for

his cigarettes when he saw the stealthy movement of a hat. It showed above cars on the extreme right, coming towards the building. If that belongs to a browser, Apple thought, he's got an odd style.

Quickly, Apple looked to the pack's other far lane, on the left. He saw the semi-expected: another hat, one that was moving in the same direction and at the same covert pace as the first. The semi-expected happened again on the hat's wearer coming into view above a sports car. It was Flaco.

Apple stepped away from the window. Turning, he looked thoughtfully at the door through which the girl had left. As he looked, the door opened.

The girl came in. She was smiling. "I found out what Mr. Jolly paid for number eighteen this morning," she said. "Three hundred pounds."

"That's a help."

"If I were you I'd offer him twenty per cent profit. He likes a fast turnover."

Three hundred and sixty pounds was more than Apple had in his account, he knew. But full payment would be days away, if the offer was accepted.

"Right," he said. "And thank you."

After a fast glance out of the window (Flaco and Gordo were steadily approaching the building), Apple got out his cheque-book and began to write quickly.

Producing an envelope, the girl said, "I hope I don't tell Mr. Jolly about you being born in it. He hates sentiment. You just never know with me."

Apple put his cheque in the envelope, on the flap of which he scribbled his name and address. He asked, "Is there a back way out of here?"

Wearing dark glasses and a quiet, mischievous smile, Josef stood waiting outside the post office in Muswell Hill.

He was ten minutes early. Apple liked that, being himself a believer in promptness.

Added to his success in eluding Flaco and Gordo at the car lot, plus the other smooth stages in this operation, the fact of the old singer having showed up, before time to boot, put Apple at the top of his spirits.

He mused that he was getting more like a pro every day. He mused on it several times. Worriedly, he wondered why.

Stopping in the roadway beside parked cars, Apple pomped the horn and waved. Josef saw him. He came over in a careful, old-man walk like a moonlighting waiter, opened the door and got in.

He asked, "Is the colour of this car really a wise choice, comrade?"

"Yes, comrade. It's far too blatant to bring its driver under suspicion. You must see that."

"Oh. Yes."

"You may smoke," Apple said, still in the same cool tone. It surprised him. He wondered what he thought he was playing at.

Josef brought out a packet of cigarettes. "Care for one? They're not Russian, sad to say. I've used up the supply I brought with me."

Apple made an airy gesture. "No, thanks. Cigarettes I can take or leave."

"You're lucky, comrade."

"Not at all, comrade. It's simply a matter of will-power. Myself, I'm not a person to allow himself to be ruled by a flippancy."

"I am," Josef said, all serene, flicking on a lighter. "And I always have been." He put flame to his cigarette and puffed as eagerly as a boy behind a barn.

Apple drove on, surging away in a manner that was so

uncharacteristic of him that his worry increased. It was now almost on a level with his cheerfulness.

"So," Josef said. It was a question.

"So, comrade?"

"You wanted to talk to me."

Apple said, "I did, and I will. There's a time and place for everything." He was disturbed to hear a tough-guy grittiness in his voice.

"This isn't it, comrade?"

"Might be. I need to wait a little while to make sure that we're not being listened to in some way."

The old man shuffled himself cozy, crossed his legs, poised his cigarette. "Ah, the joys of undercover work."

"This is no joke, comrade."

"Not to you perhaps."

The car went in and out of a pot-hole. Apple's head hit the roof with a thunk. The oath he thought to counter the pain was one he had never thought before. It had a strength and connotation of which he disapproved. He produced a milder one, then repeated the other.

Josef asked in a tone of interest, "Do you always drive like this in Britain, comrade?"

Apple looked at the speedometer. Its needle was wobbling on sixty. He warned himself that it would never do to get involved with the police again. Nodding, he lowered his foot slightly on the accelerator.

"Yes," he said. He supposed with resignation that sooner or later he would find out what was going on in his mind. His concern had reached par with his cheer.

In a less casual tone, Josef asked, "Where, comrade, are we going?"

A good question, Apple mused. Where *am* I going? He said, "Somewhere where we can talk freely."

"We're doing that now, it seems to me."

Apple grunted like a hero in a film and moved the muscles in his jaw. He wondered if he was sickening for something. That made him look in the rear-view mirror, examine his face.

He was startled to see narrowed eyes, a taut nose, a mouth pulled wide with toughness, a jutted chin. The cheery half of him said he looked ridiculous.

Josef tossed his cigarette out of the window. He asked in a slow monotone that was rich in suspicion, "Why don't we stop somewhere, perhaps have a drink?"

"The pubs are closed, comrade. Surely you must have learned about British licensing hours during your stay."

"Three days isn't long, comrade."

"Long enough, comrade."

"If you say so, comrade."

"I do, comrade," Apple said. He swung the Mazda at speed around a corner, causing the tyres to screech like tickled maids. Straightening, he held the steering-wheel with one careless hand. He took another look in the mirror. His face was more ridiculous-looking.

After rounding the next corner, Apple found the answer. He saw that he was aiming in the direction of Notting Hill.

Worry and cheer fought it out inside Apple as he realized that he was going to work the snatch, take Josef to the house in Pater Road.

Proud and aghast, Apple poured on the speed.

I can do it, he thought. I'm tough. I'm no longer a soppy amateur. I can pull off this caper and make myself forever in the service. Be a name. Be the agent who succeeded despite his drawbacks.

REMARKS in mind, Apple laughed harshly.

Josef asked a jerked, "What?"

"I was remembering, comrade. An amusing incident that happened when I was working on what's known as the Lisbon Affair. An espionage operation, I hardly need add."

Complimenting himself on his shrewdness, Apple went on to poach an Eric Ambler plot. The story would keep Josef's mind occupied, away from suspicion.

Apple drove quickly, talked with clipped words and ruthless tone, held the steering-wheel lightly, glanced in the mirror from time to time at his narrowed eyes, and stood apart from the battle between his emotions.

Josef was silent, except for saying at one point, "Sounds like a book I once read."

The Mazda came into Notting Hill. Apple, falling silent, twisted and careened along residential streets. He sat tense, mind and emotions frozen. Numbly he watched the way ahead as a final turn brought the car into Pater Road.

Apple slowed. He picked out the miniature poplars in the garden of the safe-house. They came implacably closer.

Josef said, "Something wrong, comrade?"

Only vaguely aware of the question, Apple reduced speed still more. He was almost level with the house. He tapped his foot on the brake pedal. The car slowed to a crawl.

Apple came opposite the gate. His foot touched the brake, twitched away and slammed down on the accelerator; his face straightened; his free hand came to join the wheel-clasp in the approved fashion; his worry fled and his cheer flung up its arms.

Suddenly turning to Josef, Apple said with an apologetic smile, "What was that again, please? I didn't quite catch it. Sorry. Do forgive me."

There were women with blue hair and white fingers eating pink cakes with silver bobbles. Eyes closed at the same time as mouths on each new bite, but otherwise caressed the oddly matched pair of men at the corner table.

Josef had taken off his dark glasses with the arrival of the tea and pastries. Looking unsuspicious and satisfied, he leisurely stirred his cup while pondering which cake to take. He had been granted first choice.

Apple had got over his regret for what might have been and for what probably would never be; had, in fact, turned his last-second action in Pater Road into a success, a victory of reason over brute force. He was affable.

Now, Apple stopped willing Josef to ignore the one with shaved chocolate on top, raised his cup and said, "To begin with, I am not with the KGB."

Josef's concentration on the pastries wavered, but held. He said, "Oh?"

"That, if you recall, was an assumption on your part, and I let you own it for the time being."

"I do recall."

Apple said, "Furthermore, I'm not even Russian." He sipped his tea. "Nor have I ever been in the Union of Soviet Socialist Republics." He sipped again. "Can't say I'm terribly keen to go there, either."

Josef gave him his attention, eyes coming last from the cakes. He showed his false teeth. "Your Russian is perfect."

"I lived with a Russian-speaking family when I was a child, out on the Canadian prairies. The language came to me in the form of a gift."

"I wouldn't mind a gift myself. Of information. What, in fine, is this all about?"

Apple said, "Well, freedom, I suppose."

The old man's face had become inscrutable. After pouring tea into his saucer, he sipped it empty in polite silence and said, "You're the host. I'll listen."

"Have a cake."

"I'm trying to make up my mind. Some cakes just aren't what they seem. One has to be careful."

"That's nothing but the truth, Josef. And please call me Jim, by the way."

"All right, Jim," the old man said, saucering tea. "Are you a spy or something sordid like that?"

Apple chuckled. "Can you see me as a spy?"

"Frankly, no."

Ending his chuckle, Apple took the cake with shaved chocolate on top. He said, "I belong to a private organization. You probably know of a fictional character called the Scarlet Pimpernel."

"Yes. Baroness Orczy was the author. Her character was a putrid, interfering sod who went around saving aristos from the guillotine."

"He thought he was doing the right thing. But that's what we all think, isn't it?"

"I imagine so. But don't lose the thread."

Apple said, "Our organization is called Pimpernel White. It has only one aim, and that is to assist people to escape from behind the Iron Curtain."

"And what might that be?" Josef asked, selecting a cake. It was an insipid pink thing with some of its silver bobbles missing, Apple noted wryly as, starting with Winston Churchill, he began to explain the term that was largely unknown in Russia.

By the time he had finished, Josef had eaten his cake. He drank tea to swill down crumbs and next selected a yellow deal with scalloped edges.

After taking a bite of his cake with the shaved chocolate on top, which was delicious, Apple started to paint a lavish, idealistic picture of life in the West. He gave it a gilt frame. He named famous defectors. He told how even the unknown had been helped to find liberty and happiness on this side of the Curtain. He invented wildly. He finished his cake.

Pushing away his crockery, Josef said, "And what, Jim—or Tom or Fred or Bill—has all of that to do with me?" He grinned. "Hypothetical question."

"Of course, Josef."

"So. Let us therefore stop being coy."

"By all means."

The old man stated, "You want me to defect."

"I want what you want," Apple said. "I'm simply offering you the opportunity and my help. If you should be inclined to make your life a thing of quality, I can show you how to go about it. You might otherwise find it difficult or get handed back to your own people."

Josef got out cigarettes. He lit one in lazy fashion. Sitting comfortably, he puffed smoke and sent a benign gaze around the tea-shoppe.

Apple asked, "What do you think?"

The folk singer said, "I think you're naive."

"To believe that the West has so much to offer?"

"No. To believe that anyone would swallow your story without question." He grinned again. "Oh, I don't mean the Pimpernel White nonsense. If you really are British, you could still be a spy."

"I suppose I could," Apple said. "But if I'm not British, what am I?"

"You don't understand?"

"No, Josef, I don't."

"You could, after all, be KGB. This could be a clumsy attempt at entrapment. It's quite common. The trap, not the clumsiness. You could be new at the job."

"I haven't done this particular part of the business before, I'll admit."

Josef said, "What I'm getting at, Jim, is this. If you wanted to encourage someone to defect, you'd have to prove to him that you weren't a KGB agent."

"Well, that shouldn't be too difficult."

"Really? Think about it, Jim. What, exactly, would you do to dispel the someone's doubts?"

Taking his time, Apple got out a cigarette and lit up. He felt fatly confident. This began to slim as he smoked on and found himself unable to come up with a workable idea. At last he said:

"But, of course, any solution that came from me would be suspect, because, if I were KGB, it would be something that I knew I could manage to bring off."

"A good point," Josef acknowledged. "So it would have to come from the someone. And be something that the KGB couldn't possibly arrange. That, I can assure you, in case you don't know, narrows the field to a very small paddock indeed."

"Yes, I dare say the Soviet espionage people are pretty clever," Apple said. "So okay, let's pretend that you're the someone, Josef. You tell me how I can prove I'm genuine."

"All right," the old man said, reaching for the teapot. "I'll mull it over. Care for another drop, Jim?"

They had more tea. Apple, confident again, sipped in relaxed enjoyment. He told himself that the situation was developing far beyond expectations. He also told himself that here he was, a spy, casually taking tea in a polite cafe with a Russian citizen. Apple let his eyelids grow heavy.

"Yes," Josef said. He put down his saucer. "I believe I have the answer."

"Good for you."

"Have you heard of Anna Schmidt?"

"Of course," Apple said, perking with surprise. "She's a brilliant pianist. I have a ticket for her concert tomorrow night, as it happens."

"At which time we Soviet visitors will be having a farewell banquet at a hotel. We leave for the airport and home immediately afterwards."

"So soon?"

"Yes. But to young Anna. She, you may have heard, is

violently opposed to Communism. Foolish child. There would be no way the KGB could influence her, and I can't see how they could use coercion."

"Nor can I."

"Therefore," Josef said, "to provide iron-bond evidence that you're everything you claim to be, all you have to do is get Anna Schmidt to cancel tomorrow night's performance."

Apple shook his head. "Impossible for *anyone* to arrange a thing like that."

"I don't see why it should be. Quite the reverse, it would seem. Easy for a noble-minded group, one whose aims are against everything that Anna Schmidt holds cheap. She would be delighted to oblige."

"No, Josef. It would be impossible."

The old man showed his dentures. "Then that means I made the right choice. Almost anything else would still be suspect." He reached for his dark glasses. "And now it's time I was getting back."

Apple thought about it.

He churned the whole thing over while taking Josef to a drop-off point near Peace Manor, while driving home, while changing into his track suit, and while traumalessly sneaking Monico out for an early run.

He was still thinking about it.

In the car, when Apple had tried to revive the subject, hoping to get agreement on a more obtainable proof, Josef had said, "Come on, Jim, don't make me suspicious." Getting out, he had paused as if in cogitation, but when he had spoken it was only to ask, mock plaintively, "Was that chocolate cake as good as it looked?"

Apple ran at a lope. It took no conscious effort. He was hardly aware of the street or of Monico bounding on ahead.

His mind was busy with the questions that came closer to finding answers on every asking.

Would Josef defect? Apple concluded now that the fact of the old man not saying he was interested in defection was entirely irrelevant. How could he say such a thing when talking to someone who might be KGB? And if he wasn't interested, why had he suggested proof?

Progress was being made, Apple thought. His lope took on a bounce.

Could an approach be made to Anna? No comment.

How could such an approach be made? Not a clue, except that it would have to be personal, not arranged through Upstairs, and have all the drama necessary for full impact.

More progress, Apple told himself. He became less out of touch with his surroundings, to the extent of noting that Monico was backing away from a yappy little dog while a man was calling out, "Chicken!" When he drew closer, Apple told the fool coldly that it was not a matter of courage, it was just that Monico wasn't terribly interested in being a dog.

How could Anna be located? As easily as falling off a baby grand. One called the theatre or a newspaper or London Music Week's organizers—and asked, explaining that one wanted to know because one wanted to send the lady a gift of roses in appreciation of her talent and fortitude.

Another notch for progress, Apple thought, stepping up his pace. The list of questions was shrinking.

Would Anna cooperate? The answer to that being unknown, the question was inadmissible. It was no longer listed.

If cooperate Anna did, what excuse could she give for cancellation of her concert? A good one, that. It ought to wait until the last was not only back on the list but answered with an affirmative.

Yet Apple persevered with this question. He was intrigued with the idea that it wasn't what could be used that mattered, but what could not. It had to be KGB-unfixable—as it would be judged by Josef.

Sickness was out, Apple mused; a clever Hammer would have little trouble in putting a drug into Anna's food, drink, atmosphere. Accident was out; the KGB were the best in the game at that business of making a planned attack look like mishap. Damaged piano was out; obviously. Fire or other catastrophe in the theatre was out; same reason.

Increasing his speed still more, Apple realized that he had named most of the possibilities, usable or not. The sole remaining idea that occurred to him was cancellation because of the death of a loved one.

But Anna Schmidt was an unmarried orphan without siblings, and no romantic attachments had been mentioned in press releases.

Apple dropped it there. He thought he could come back to the problem later, if he should be so lucky for it to be necessary. That left another question: was there any other way of bringing the kidnap/defection caper to fruition?

No. It was Anna Schmidt or nothing.

So, final question, was he going to try it? Of course he was. That was why he had brought Monico out two hours early, to give himself the time. And time was a vital factor. Josef would be out of reach soon after the concert, or non-concert.

Apple came to a fast stop. He whistled to Monico, turned and began to race back at full pelt.

"Take it off."

"Not the lot, surely."

"Almost. Leave a bit. I don't want to be naked."

"I hope you know what you're doing, sir," the barber said. Middle-aged, he had flowing grey hair and the sad eyes of a man at the end of a hand-out queue.

Apple said, "I do. I want the shortest crew cut you've got in stock." He laughed. He told himself to remember that one.

The barber sighed. "It's your hair, sir." He tapped comb and scissors together. "Here goes."

"As quickly as you can, please."

"Yes, sir. And what would you like with it? I can give you football, television, pigeon-racing or Chinese poetry."

"To be honest," Apple said, "I'd prefer to think. Sorry. Some other time."

"After I get through," the barber said, "another time'll be a long way off." He set to work.

After his run, a quick shower and a change back to normal clothes, Apple had telephoned an ex-girl-friend who worked in a record store. She sold pop and listened secretly to the classics, whose performers were her idols. Apple had learned from her that Anna Schmidt had a male cousin in Frankfurt.

Next, Apple had called London Music Week's publicity department. From it he had learned that Anna was staying at the Richway Hotel on Park Lane.

Before leaving the flat for the barber-shop, Apple had eaten four slices of toast with lemon marmalade.

Now, having gone over once again the story he intended to use, he assured himself that his concoction had all the right elements. Anna needed to accept placidly, not be joyous or scared or excited, so that if things went awry she wouldn't be unhappy or shocked or disappointed.

Lips compressed, the barber snipped busily. He was nearly finished. The gingery hair was half an inch long and standing as if in tired annoyance, like an old brush that had been rubbed the wrong way. Looking at himself in the mirror, Apple decided that he looked definitely German. He felt grateful.

He asked, "Have you seen the new panel show on telly?"

That kept them chatting until cloth-off time, kept the barber from looking overly distressed by his creation. He managed an apologetic smile for the tip.

Leaving, Apple went to an underground garage near Harlequin Mansions. He drove out in the Mazda, its redness cherrylike from a wash. That Ethel didn't keep coming into his mind Apple thought a splendid indication of his emotional stability.

Minutes later, Apple was drawing up on the forecourt of the mammoth Richway Hotel. As he got out, full of the confidence which comes from feeling that failure is certain, therefore needn't be worried about, a large doorman strode forward in his flashing finery, face grim.

Apple slammed the car door. He lifted his Bloomsbury Billiards Club card into view fleetingly and said, "Don't let this car out of your sight, old man. There've been three this week."

Stopping, eyeing Apple's height, the doorman asked, "Three what?"

"Booby-trap bombs in cars," Apple said crisply. "IRA jobs. But we're keeping it out of the press, so mum's the word, eh?" Not waiting to watch the reaction he went on into the hotel.

Its lobby was big enough to lose a child in. The people who were sitting, wandering, or browsing at the row of open-fronted shops looked as though they had never heard of children.

Apple marched like a guardsman over to the reception desk, where he rapped for an attention that he already owned, that he'd had during the latter part of his approach.

One of the three clerks won the discreet jostle, arrived opposite him and looked up with hope-of-drama eyes.

Voice lowered, implying that this wasn't for just any old body, Apple said, "I wish to speak to Miss Schmidt, please." He nodded. "An official matter."

All hope, the clerk lifted a telephone receiver. He dialled while asking, "Your name, sir?"

"Schmidt also."

After murmuring into the handset, the clerk handed it over with, "Miss Schmidt, Mr. Schmidt." He moved three inches along the counter.

A female voice asked lightly, "Is this a joke?"

Apple spoke in German. "No, but it does sound funny. In fact, this whole thing is a little odd."

"How nice to hear German again," Anna Schmidt said in that language. "What whole thing?"

"Well, I'm here at the request of your cousin in Frankfurt, and the first oddness is that he won't let me use his name." Apple didn't know it. "Does he always act as crazy as that?"

Anna Schmidt laughed. "I don't know. But boys of seventeen do get strange ideas."

So now I have his age, Apple thought while watching the clerk give up and move away bleakly. He said, "We'll call him Kurt, shall we?"

"No, let's not make it worse. Hans is fine."

Smugly: "Fair enough. But the message I have for you from Hans has to be delivered in person. I can't break my word on that. Shall I come up, or would you prefer to meet me here in the lobby?"

"Oh. I don't know."

Craftily: "I think down here would be best. After all, you don't know me from Adam."

"Yes, all right. Five minutes."

So far so surprising, Apple thought, wandering away from the desk. But surely the complete deal couldn't possibly work. Of course it couldn't.

Relaxed with confidence, Apple positioned himself near the bank of lifts.

When from one of these Anna Schmidt appeared, Apple noted happily that she was on the tall side, also that her face was prettier and less severe than in her photographs. He felt more smitten than ever.

Anna wore a summery skirt as brightly and haphazardly coloured as discarded ice-cream wrappers. Her top was a man's shirt, though no male could ever have managed to poke out the chest in so abundant a way.

Tossing back her long dark hair, the pianist came forward. Apple met her with his hand out. "How do you do. I'm Adolf Schmidt." With the handshake he bowed and clicked his heels mutedly.

The girl smiled. "Hello. I love your formality. But I'll call you Adolf, if you don't mind." She used the familiar form. "And you must call me Anna. You're marvellously tall."

"So are you."

Talking casually, they moved over to a couch and sat. Apple was so satisfied, complacent, that he felt momentarily at a loss when Anna asked:

"What's the message from crazy Hans?"

Recovering, Apple said, "He wants to see you. Now. At once."

"You mean he's here in Britain? Hans?"

"Yes. In the country, a short drive from here. He's acting paranoid, but I think he's just piling on the melodrama. You know what they're like at that age."

"I'll say I do. But what's the problem?"

"Search me, Anna. I thought maybe you'd have a better idea than I have."

She shrugged. "Got himself into some kind of a mess, I imagine. Money or a girl."

"That sounds like Hans."

"Or he's fallen out again with his foster-parents, who, actually, are rather nice."

"He wouldn't agree with that."

Anna shook her head. "That Hans."

"Whatever the problem," Apple said. "Will you come? I have a car outside. I can take you."

Anna placed a long, slender forefinger on the cleft in her chin and looked thoughtfully at the floor. Apple almost hoped she would decline, so he could tell himself he had told himself so.

"All right," Anna said. She got up. "I'm a great one for family duty."

Next, they were outside, where the doorman was standing on the farthest edge of the forecourt. They got in the car, on which Anna commented, "What a glorious colour."

Starting the motor, Apple thought how pleasant it was that Anna was no fanatic in her anti-Communism. His smittenship thrived.

As hc drove off, Apple glanced automatically in the rear-view mirror. Hurrying forward in the distance were two men. Although they were blurred by the double movement, theirs and the car's, Apple could make out that one was fat and the other thin.

The journey, as he saw it, was necessary only as filling, like bread in a sausage. It would spread the time between meeting each other cold and the presentation of his concocted story, making for a more likely acceptance. A stronger familiarity would further help.

Until the traffic began to lose its density and fuss, like fans dispersing from a stadium, Apple and Anna were mostly silent, merely making idle comments on the passing scene.

At length Apple said, "You know, Anna, it's good of you to come away at a moment's notice. Especially with a complete stranger."

She glanced at him with perked head and a smile. "Oh, I don't know. You look respectable enough to me."

"Ah." He changed gear brutally.

"How long have you been in London, Adolf?"

Apple fabricated easily on that one, before getting to a question of his own, which he asked not only to get the subject off his invented self but also for personal reasons.

"What was it like, Anna, making your dash for freedom at the checkpoint?"

"Everyone asks me about that."

He waggled his hand. "Forget I mentioned it. Poor you, you must be bored to death with the repetition."

Impulsively she turned to him and flicked a touch on his arm. "No. Sorry. I don't mind telling you. I haven't talked about it for a long time, due to always putting people off with an excuse."

After they had shared a smile, which made Apple's lower spine itch, Anna began to tell of her adventure, starting with the careful planning.

Apple listened in fascination. He clenched the steering-wheel tightly to match Anna's tension as the time for her escape drew near; sweated under the chin while she strolled her pedal bicycle in a casual manner towards the checkpoint; twitched when she suddenly flung herself onto the machine; held his breath as the East German guards fired their rifles at the madly pedalling figure; slumped with painful relief when the other barrier was safely reached.

Apple calmed himself with a cigarette while Anna talked on, describing her new life and her climb as a pianist. Next the shared subject became music in general.

Being a fan of the whole spectrum, King Oliver to the

Queen's College Choir, Apple was able to hold his own. He forgot the whyfor of the situation.

It came fully to him with a slap, however, as he drove along the last stretch of lane. "Here we are," he said, his voice a nervous grate.

The cottage stood alone. It had no style other than mock-ancient. Built out of old material in the thirties, it spread along on one floor and bulged at the corners. The bow window was so cute that Apple intended doing something about it one of these days.

He handed Anna out of the car and took her inside. She looked smilingly around the small parlour with its beams, chintz and brassware.

"Heavens," she said. "It's so British."

Apple took a deep breath. He said, in English, "As a matter of fact, Anna, so am I."

Several seconds passed before Anna turned towards him. She did so in slow motion. Looking at him blankly she said, also switching from German to English, "I don't understand you."

"I'm going to explain."

"And where's Hans? I'd almost forgotten about him."

"Would you—er—like to sit down?"

She went on looking at him steadily. "Not right now, thank you."

Apple clasped his hands like a humble suppliant. "My name is not Adolf Schmidt," he said. "I am not German. I had my hair cut this way no more than an hour ago. I have never met your cousin and didn't know his name or age until you told me yourself."

Anna folded her arms in a manner that suggested protection, at the same time taking a small step backwards. She shook her head, saying a bemused, "What?"

"The door's not locked, Anna. Also the car's open and has the key in the ignition. You're free to go and drive yourself back, if you wish."

"I still don't . . ."

"Anna," Apple said. "I've been lying to you all along. I got you here under false pretences."

Her blankness faded. Head on one side, she gazed at him with so potent a disappointment, so obvious a degree of illusions destroyed, that Apple cringed.

Next, he started to blush.

The heat came up from his knees. It singed his groin, scorched his belly, seared his chest, baked his neck and, with a final rush, came into burning place on his face. He felt as though he were suffocating. The blush attack was one of the worst he had ever experienced.

Jerkily he turned away so that, unseen, he could give himself totally to the battle, create the scene.

The water is unbearably hot. Nevertheless, he has to bear it. His hands and feet being tied, there's no way he can get out of the big black pot. All he can do is stare pleadingly at the cannibal chieftain, who is humming to himself as he sprinkles rosemary on the steaming water.

The picture shimmied at the interruption of an alien noise. Distantly Apple recognized it as the sound of the door latch being lifted. With a mental shrug he returned himself to the jungle scene.

The heat is fierce, his fear is raging. He tries to keep his mind from the immediate future, his eyes from the witch doctor who is sharpening a knife. Every member of the tribe, from toddler to crone, is showing pointed teeth.

Gradually Apple cooled. The picture did a slow fade as he returned to a state of normality. He sighed, wiped the dampness from his brow, turned around.

Anna was still there. She stood beside the door, one hand on its latch. Dropping the hand, she asked:

"What method do you use?"

Anna Schmidt had been a blusher since the early teens. Her condition, like Apple's, was at the *grand mal* level. She had tried psychoanalysis and hypnotism, acupuncture and various tranquillizers. She had written to advice columns in periodicals. She had bought cures through advertisements. She had been to quacks, herbalists and white witches. She still blushed.

The story of her travail she related in the kitchen, where she and Apple got in each other's way while making coffee. She called him Nick. He had reintroduced himself as Nick Morgan. It was one of the names he would have liked to have owned, along with Rod Strike and Dirk Brash. He had added, however, "It's not my real name, but I prefer it to Adolf."

With mugs of coffee they went back to the parlour and sat in facing rocking-chairs. In her faint Canadian accent, Anna said in conclusion:

"My sole consolation over the years has been the uncertain knowledge that blushers are supposed to be more decent than the average."

"Is that so?"

She nodded. "Which is nice, 'cos I've always thought I was a bit of a bitch."

Apple laughed. He said, "But to get back to methods. I tried my first as a boy. A doctor told me I needed to give myself confidence with an accomplishment. I took up languages. It didn't help in the slightest."

"Maybe not, but your German is fabulous."

Which returned them to the present situation. They cleared their throats and looked around the room.

Finishing his coffee, Apple set the mug down at his feet and leaned forward. He said:

"I brought you here to spin you a story, Anna. It has a lot of bathos and human-interest stuff, and it was intended to pull your heart-strings, as a way of winning your cooperation."

Her head back against the chair, Anna rocked gently. She asked, "Your own invention?"

"All my own. But I don't think it'd win any prizes, even if there was a violin weeping in the background."

Apple went on to tell about a little girl, dangerously ill, who was a rabid fan of Anna Schmidt's. A pianist herself, it was believed she would improve greatly if she could meet Anna and hear her play.

"On getting your agreement," Apple said, "I call the parents to say we're on our way, only to be told that the girl is in a coma. That's the end of it. I take you home."

"To await scene two?"

"Exactly. Which would be tomorrow night, at seven o'clock. Then, the child becomes conscious, though on the point of death. She stands a chance of rallying, her doctor thinks, if she could get a visit from her idol."

Anna smiled around, "God, Nick, it's terrible."

"Agreed. I'm so glad I didn't try it on you."

"But this is the crux, isn't it? Tomorrow night at seven."

"That's when your performance is due to start," Apple said. "My hope was that you would cancel it and come with me to see this invented child."

"Sorry," Anna said. "I'm lost."

Apple set his own chair rocking. He said, "I work for an organization that's dedicated to damaging the Marxist philosophy. This is done in many, many ways, from the subtle to the blatant. At the moment, cancellation of the Anna Schmidt performance is the aim."

"Oh really?"

"I can't tell you why, just as I can't tell you anything about the organization, or about myself."

"But you are telling the truth now, I think."

"I am, Anna. The Communists would be damaged if tomorrow's piano recital didn't come off. However, it would have to be done in such a way that didn't hint at outside interference." He went on to outline the non-usable reasons for calling off the performance.

Anna listened with watchful care. Slowly, her chair got into rhythm with the rocking of Apple's. She looked quietly troubled as well as intrigued.

Apple said, "And that's the complete picture, or as much of it as I can give you."

"You could be working for a musical rival, of course."

"I could, yes. I never thought of that."

"But I don't believe you are," Anna said. "There'd be an easier way than all this."

"A dozen at least."

"You could also be a Red yourself, wanting the concert cancelled for some involved reason."

Apple said, "That's true."

"Except that I feel Moscow would use a different type of intermediary. Meaning, I suppose, a non-blusher."

"I'll buy that."

"So all right," Anna said, "let's say that you belong to one of those eccentric English groups who take militant action against things that they consider to be wrong. It's feasible. Where else but in Britain would antivivisectionists blow up a laboratory? Which is what happened here a couple of months ago, I heard."

"And will happen again."

"Yet it won't change anything. Not in the long run. Nor would my skipping the recital tomorrow night have any long-term effect. Or would it? Honestly."

Apple lifted his hands, dropped them back in his lap. "I don't know," he said.

"Thank you."

"But then, there's so little I do know about this affair. I'm only a minion. All I am sure of is that every drop helps to fill the bucket."

"Or," Anna suggested, "it could be that this is just one piece in a jigsaw?"

"It could. There might be others like myself working on different bits of the same puzzle."

"And if the completed picture showed the destruction of Communism—that would be very pretty."

"Communism can't be destroyed, Anna," Apple said. "But it can be contained."

After that, there was silence for a while, except for the faint squeak from the two chairs rocking in time. Apple felt pleased and hopeful. The former was in respect of the caper, Anna and his view of her knees; the latter was more or less the same.

Anna sighed. She said, "I'd like to help your cause. Love to. But I have to balance effects. Would the Red damage outweigh the damage created by cancellation? Think of all the people who'd be hurt. Those involved in the arrangements that have been going on for months. Those who've come from far away, in some cases from abroad, to hear me play. Hundreds and hundreds of people. It wouldn't be fair."

"Yes, I see what you mean."

"I don't think I could do it, Nick. Also, I don't know of any reason to give for not playing, apart from those you mentioned, which won't do."

Apple said, "I do realize that it's asking a great deal. But I had to try."

Anna asked with a frown, "You won't lose your job or anything, will you?"

Smiling thanks, Apple shook his head. "No. I'll just go down a couple of pegs, whereas if I'd succeeded I would have earned myself a little glory."

"I'm sorry."

"But listen, Anna. Think it over during the next twenty-four hours. Both the cancellation and a way of doing it, neatly for the cause, savingly for you. I sincerely believe that it would create a great deal of distress in Moscow."

Anna stopped her chair and got up. "All right. That's the least I can do. But please don't hold out much hope. I'm ninety-nine per cent sure that the answer has to be in the negative."

"One per cent is better than no bread—or something," Apple said, also rising. He stepped to the door, drew it wide. "I have a stronger hope, however. Which is that you might like to stop on the way back and have a drink."

"Ninety-nine per cent affirmative. The one is there because you may try to work at persuasion."

Apple shook his head. "As of this moment, the subject of the concert is taboo. I just clocked out."

The one drink became two. Anna had draught beer, Apple sherry on the rocks. Although the village pub didn't serve meals, the landlady was happy to provide sandwiches of home-cured ham, along with pickled onions and red cabbage. It was such a moveable feast that they moved a repeat.

The locals, who looked suspiciously like city commuters in bucolic drag, were in Friday-night mood. When their search for a piano-player became desperate, Apple urged Anna to volunteer, which he could tell she was itching to do.

Unrecognized, Anna sat at the wall-supported upright and thundered out the standard sing-alongs. Apple winced for her fingers.

After a final drink, they left and headed for town. They sang German beer hall refrains all the way, competing to produce the most obscure songs. Apple let Anna win.

At the hotel entrance he clicked his heels, kissed her hand and said, "I don't imagine we'll meet again."

"Why not?"

"Well . . ."

"At ten o'clock tomorrow night," Anna said, "there'll be

a small, post-recital supper here. If you're not prostrate with disappointment by that time, please come."

Again Apple said, "Well . . ."

"Good night, Nick or whoever. Thank you for a most unusual evening."

"The pleasure was all mine."

Anna said, "I know I'm flattering myself outrageously, but I have to ask this. Was all the connivance merely for you to get to know me?"

Though tempted to lie, Apple had to say, "No, I'm afraid not. I've been honest with you. Please think over what I want to happen."

"But that's a taboo subject," Anna said. She twirled away with a wave and went inside.

The subject stayed taboo with Apple himself during the short ride to Bloomsbury, where he parked in the underground garage. His thoughts were on a personal mission—Anna Schmidt. He realized that he had reached point eight on the smitten scale.

Climbing the stairs in Harlequin Mansions, Apple did come close to breaking his taboo, but only insofar as thinking of how cleverly he had managed to win Anna's confidence. She believed in him. Anything could happen.

After losing two falls out of three to Monico, Apple headed for his bedroom. He stopped on a lurch at a jingle of ringing. One ring came from the flat doorbell, the other from the telephone.

"One moment, please," Apple called along the hall. He supposed that, as usual, it would be Mrs. 3B wanting to borrow a cup of sugar or a twist of tea, an onion or two slices of bread.

In the living-room he lifted the telephone receiver. A male voice that was unfamiliar asked, "Is that One?"

"It better be," Apple said, gamely trying out the pro's flippant attitude. He blinked and added, "Yes."

"Think of a number."

After Apple had chanted his service identity number the man said, "The tourists are going sightseeing again tomorrow, at one o'clock. It'll be their last outing."

The doorbell rang again. Covering the mouthpiece Apple yelled, "All right, all right." He took his hand away and asked, "Where're the tourists going?"

"Imperial War Museum. It's in the Lambeth Road."

"I know, and in the building that used to be a hospital for the insane, called Bethlehem, which was corrupted to Bethlem, and then came into the language as *bedlam*."

The man said drily, "That's fascinating, One."

"Well, I think it is."

"From there the tourists will be going to make the traditional visit to Karl Marx's grave. We have that as firm."

"And the museum trip?"

"Fairly firm," the man said. "It was reported in this evening's newspaper."

Apple asked, "What comes after the cemetery?" He tried to sound as if it mattered.

"Nothing. Over and out, as we spooks say."

Cradling the receiver, Apple hurried to the apartment door, which he opened and swung wide. On seeing his landlord he said, "Oh. Good evening." He hoped Monico would stay put in the living-room.

"Evening, Mr. Porter," Charles Lampton said, eyes stolid in his craggy face. "Sorry to interrupt you in the middle of something important."

"There was a pan on the stove I couldn't leave," Apple said. "What can I do for you, Mr. Lampton?"

Adjusting the lapels of his droopy green suit, the landlord let his body drift to one side, in order to see beyond Apple, who then leaned neatly in the same direction.

"I called, Mr. Porter, to make sure I haven't been giving out false information, born of ignorance."

"I'm afraid I'm not with you, Mr. Lampton."

"You might, for all I know, have a guest."

"A guest?"

"In a manner of speaking," the landlord said, coming erect. He continued his movement and swayed in the other direction.

Apple did the same. "I'm still not with you."

"The matter, Mr. Porter, concerns a dog."

Apple felt a stab of fear, which he allowed to show on his face as astonishment. "A dog, Mr. Lampton?" he said. "But domestic pets are not allowed in Harlequin Mansions. And quite right, too."

The landlord straightened. "I thought, you see, Mr. Porter, that it was always possible that, in a weak moment, feeling kind, you had agreed to give board and lodgings to a friend's dog for a few days."

"No, no, no. I? Not at all. Never."

"It would be understandable. Weak moment. Kind. Board and lodgings. Friend. Few days."

Apple shook his head slowly, as if in remonstration. "Rules are rules, Mr. Lampton."

"Oh, I agree."

"One can take friendship too far."

Charles Lampton tried craning up on tiptoe; but, Apple being too tall, he sagged again with a sour expression. He said, "Then I was not giving out false information."

"To whom, Mr. Lampton?"

"The two gentlemen who called on me this evening."

"Oh yes?" Apple said, wondering why Lampton didn't try a fast squat. "Two gentlemen?"

"They wanted to know if this house was where the tall man lived, the one who had a tall dog. I said no, there were no dogs here."

Apple, after a fast think, said, "The gentlemen are probably friends of mine. Great practical jokers. Does this sound familiar?" He went on to describe Flaco and Gordo.

"That's they," the landlord said, looking disappointed. He began to sway to the right, then, as Apple went along, made a quick switch to the extreme left.

Apple had to let him have his view. Any other course would have been too suspicious. He said, turning to glance along the hall, which was empty:

"Thank you for inadvertently letting me know about this, Mr. Lampton. Now it's my turn. I go to where they're living and ask about cats."

Looking more disappointed, the landlord mumbled, "Yes."

After Apple had closed him out with a cheery good night, he leaned back on the door and thought about it.

CHAPTER 4

Next day, when he was driving onto Waterloo Bridge among heavy noon traffic, Apple heard a thudding sound. It was next joined by a matching rhythm that he could feel in the steering-wheel.

Apple's first thought in explanation was that there were ridges in the surface of the road. But a glance showed him tarmac as smooth as his own freshly shaven chin.

Apple's second thought, which came when sound and feeling were growing rapidly stronger, made him sit as tautly erect with dread as headroom would allow.

He had remembered the booby-trap bomb story that he had given to the doorman at the Richway Hotel.

The instinctive impulse which came to Apple was to drive faster, to escape, to leave the danger behind. But he would, of course, be taking it with him. He put his foot on the brake.

As he did, the car began to jiggle with an upsurge in the thudding; and Apple recognized causation. He sagged his body and his eyelids.

Even though relieved, however, Apple was vaguely disappointed. He reflected sighingly that having a flat tyre would probably never happen to a pro.

Stopping in the kerb in the middle of the bridge, Apple set about changing wheels. In this he was hindered by the fast-passing traffic (the flat being on the off-side). But he was also able to lose his disappointment, regain some of that tingly dread, by imagining what this could mean.

The enemy, above such crude, obvious and unsophisticated methods of elimination as bombs in cars (so noisy and messy), had arranged for this particular tyre to go down in this particular place. A hit-and-run driver would be unsuspected of deep, sinister motives, and the public surface of the spy-game pond would be unrippled.

It took Apple twice as long as normal to finish the job. He felt less the non-pro as he drove on to a service station, where he washed his hands.

By that time it was past one o'clock. Apple went to the Imperial War Museum anyway, just in case. There he quickly learned from an official that the Russians had finished their visit.

They had spent it, the same official reported irately, in claiming that the Union of Soviet Socialist Republics was the home of most of the war-related inventions, starting at gunpowder, ending on missles, and collecting mutiny along the way.

"Especially that old twit who does all the gabbing," the official said.

Apple was pleased to hear evidence of Josef's playing of the Red-chauvinist and untiring propagandist. Protesting too much was always a good omen.

Apple left the souvenirs of legal, condoned bedlam and set off to drive to the other side of the city. Knowing that he would make better time than the tourist coach, he had no urgency. He wouldn't be uselessly late in reaching Highgate for a bit of play-acting in his role as kidnapper.

Reminded by the before-and-after pictures on a poster lauding a diet food, Apple, cutting into an Anastasia reverie, spared a thought for Flaco and Gordo.

Apple had come to the conclusion that the visit of the two men to Harlequin Mansions, as well as his view of them last evening near the Richway Hotel, could have been a case of, respectively, a Porter-assume and a Porter-see, which were first cousins of a Porter-catch.

The blurred running figures could have been anybody, the landlord's description of his visitors could fit a quarter of the male population in that age group.

All this had come because of Apple being able to admit that he liked the idea of being tailed; further, he enjoyed appreciating the skill that would be involved in his repeatedly being located. It was in the classic espionage mould.

Apple arrived in Highgate Village, which had somehow in this modern age managed to retain most of its charm. He found a place to park right in the square and locked up the Mazda securely.

Walking away, Apple answered a nagging question in respect of the Porter-assumed Flaco and Gordo: if they were not the real pair of tailers, why had they asked the landlord about him? Because, one, they might be interested in dogs, particularly the Ibizan Podenco.

Apple had no two to offer. Come to that, he wasn't terribly happy with one.

A sloping narrow street feeding from the south side of the village brought Apple to cemetery gates that were suitably decrepit and Gothic. Beyond them appeared to be more of the quick than the dead.

Among the graves and monuments, the statues and crypts, the headstones and ornate crosses, people were either standing to chat or strolling to view. Their clothing said that they were tourists. They had come here, Apple knew, between other obligatory sights such as Buckingham Palace and the Horse Guards Parade and the Tower of London.

Apple went through the gates onto a crumbly tarmac path. Walking in a manner which he hoped would be seen as casual to the mass, pseudo-casual to the interested, he was guided in the right direction by the concentration of people.

Soon Apple saw, over heads, the main drawing-card of the cemetery. It was a large, simple block of stone topped by a bust of Karl Marx. The father of Communism with a capital C was streaked with white. He looked as though he had been placed there strictly for the birds.

Abruptly, Apple changed manner and direction. Ducking, he turned aside. He made his face severe. In a crouch he darted off the path and into the jumble of masonry.

Several people looked at Apple with interest or worry or sympathy. He hoped that among the lookers would be Angus Watkin's One-watcher.

Apple changed to a slow lurk, which he considered to be quite effective. It took him around a stone angel with no wings left, across an unmarked grave (Apple clearing it with one huge, polite stride) and up to the rim of a studious-looking group.

About to deflect, Apple was stopped by one of the people, who asked him if he knew the location of Michael Faraday's last resting-place.

Apple took advantage of this gift, mumbling with his head lowered as though to a conspirator. He left the enquirer looking bewildered and went on, circling, keeping the Marx block as a central point.

After sliding past a shrouded urn in green marble, Apple turned to see how he was doing for observers. He found himself being stared at by only one. It was the Hammer with the ski-jump nose.

With Apple in full-face view, Gateman went through a fast change of expression. His features slid from curiosity to the familiar where-have-I-seen . . .

Apple swung around and strode on, his pace back to brisk. He continued circling as he threaded between graves and people. When at last he saw Josef, he stopped.

With the Marx block in the background, the singer was posing for a photograph, chin high and arms nobly folded. He noticed Apple, who then gave a jerk of his head. Josef replied with a faint nod.

It was ten minutes before he was able to get away from those around him, with their adoration, cameras and autograph books. On a circuitous route he ambled to where Apple was leaning against a crypt, there bending over as if he were looking at the wording.

Aside he asked, "How's Pimpernel White?"

"Fine, thank you," Apple said in a quiet voice, barely moving his lips. "We're still trying to make contact with Anna Schmidt."

"You mean she's guarded?"

"Of course not. She has all the freedom she wants, as do we all in the West. It's simply that she's incommunicado."

"That's odd."

"Not at all. Like many artistes, she likes to be alone before an important concert. Rest her body and mind."

"So nothing's arranged."

Apple murmured, "These things take time."

"And time's short," the old man said without looking up from his stoop. "We board the airport coach directly from the hotel where we're having the banquet tonight."

"What's the hotel called?"

"The Hammersmith Forge."

"Josef, you might not be on that coach."

"Never can tell, Jim."

As if idly, Apple glanced around. He caught a glimpse of Gateman moving between chunks of masonry. "Listen, Josef," he said. "Did you tell anyone about me?"

Still pretending to read, the old folk singer said, "No one who matters."

"Meaning that you told someone who doesn't?"

"Yes. My colleagues. Those three old bores. Right from the beginning. They're harmless."

"I wonder."

"I don't."

A female voice called out in broken Russian, "Oh, there you are, Josef."

The singer straightened without hurry. Smiling towards the approaching, gushy woman he said convict-style out of the corner of his mouth:

"Tonight I'll slip away from the table between courses. I'll watch the start of Anna Schmidt's recital on the television in the hotel lobby."

"Or watch the cancellation announcement," Apple said. "In which case you'll be seeing me later. So long."

He pushed away from the crypt suddenly, his face putting on a show of anger, as if the gushy woman, who had nearly arrived, were interrupting an important segment of a kidnap scheme.

For a while longer Apple went on playing for the benefit of a possible observer. Neatly he avoided Gateman, as well as two priests and a squat woman who was wearing the uniform of a bus-conductress.

At one stage, lurking between bouts of darting, Apple came face to face with Josef's colleagues. The three old men reacted like cats seeing a mouse, rearing back slightly before making to hurry forward.

Apple slipped away.

Out of the cemetery, he walked back up towards the village centre. He told himself that, all in all, he had done very well at making something out of nothing.

In the square Apple halted at a distance, alert, on seeing near his Mazda a stout male figure. Before Apple could look around for a complementing thin shape, the man turned. He was scar-marred Bill Burton.

Apple went forward again. He changed direction when the agent switched his eyes pointedly towards a pub. Which, as Bill Burton was a teetotaller, was not an invitation to join him in a drink.

At the door of the building Apple glanced back. The stout operative was nowhere to be seen. Nice dissolve, Apple thought happily, and insisted to himself that he wasn't the least bit envious. He went on in.

The saloon bar was crowded, this being the tail-end of the midday session. Every table was taken and customers stood three deep along the bar. Froth and bubbles were getting more attention than the television set.

Apple gazed around. Several seconds passed before he saw the man whom he was expecting to find here.

Angus Watkin sat at a table with two women. Watkin was his usual nondescript self. His female companions, aged about twenty-five, had brittle yellow hair like tired string, a jangle of jewellery, brassy clothes and enough cosmetics to supply a giggle of transvestites.

The three people at the table formed a picture commonplace enough to be boring: an older man buying the company of a couple of tarts.

After meeting Apple's gaze, Angus Watkin glanced at the fourth, vacant chair, then looked back at his underling and gave him the join-us office.

As he edged his way across the crowded room, Apple couldn't help wondering what his chief would have done if someone had insisted on taking that unoccupied seat. But he didn't really want to know.

At the table, Apple bowed in answer to the names which Angus Watkin, slicing his hand in air, mumbled unintelligibly, and said, "How do you do."

The two women looked up at him while giving back, in unison, "Pleased to meetcha."

It was right in accent but too metallic in timbre, Apple decided. He was surprised that his Control would use such detectable phonies, even though they might be here merely for stage dressing.

Apple sat down opposite Angus Watkin, who slid him a glass of dark liquid with ice, saying, "La Ina is the sherry that you prefer, I believe."

"It is, sir, yes," Apple said, then at once regretted his automatic giving of the *sir*. He felt sure it couldn't be kosher. But Angus Watkin appeared to be unperturbed. Apple said, "Thank you. Cheers."

They all four of them sipped. After neatly setting down his mild whisky and water, Watkin said, "I'll get straight to the matter at hand, Porter, and that is abduction."

Apple was surprised again, on two counts: at the open mention of the operation, and of the use of his name. Although there was too much noise and talk in the room for any of the other customers to catch what was being said at the small table, the two women could hear perfectly well.

Watkin asked, "Something wrong, Porter?"

"No, sir," Apple said. He was forced to the conclusion that the quasi-tarts, despite their comparative youth, must be of the elite who were familiar with Upstairs. He added, "Well, yes, actually."

"Such as?"

Apple gestured to indicate the room, his drink, the situation. "All this."

"It is not to your usual standard?"

"I'm a bit pressed for time, is what I mean, sir."

"Indeed you are," Angus Watkin said. "There's about five hours to go. And you would rather not waste any of it in social intercourse."

"Something like that, sir."

"Not to worry, Porter. I have no intentions of detaining you for long."

"Thank you, sir."

"You may smoke, if that will calm your racing nerves."

Apple nodded and delved into his pockets. "Cigarette?" he asked, looking from one woman to the other. They ignored him completely. With a vacant smile, each was intent on dunking ice. Overacted, Apple thought.

After lighting up he said, "I expect, sir, that you'd like a progress report."

"No, I would not, Porter. What I want from you is an intention report."

"Oh."

"I, in fact, will tell *you* what you have accomplished so far," Angus Watkin said. "Beginning with the first day." He went on to outline Apple's Soviet-connected activities as seen by a One-watcher, including the scene ten minutes ago at the cemetery.

Apple noted that not once did the women look up at Watkin's face; nor did they at his own when it was his turn to talk. They gave the impression of listening with care.

Therefore Apple was himself careful as he retailed his invented plan of luring one or possibly two of the old folk singers away from Peace Manor this afternoon. He gave only the skeleton, spending more time on describing the grounds and the greenhouse.

He said, "I've been there, obviously."

"I know," his chief said. "Once, at any rate."

"Twice," Applie lied airily. He stubbed out his cigarette in style. "I've been very busy."

"Not so much, Porter, that you didn't have the time to spare for romantic dalliance."

Apple lost his airiness as fast as a sneeze. "I, sir?"

"You, sir. That girl."

"Which girl?"

Watkin nodded in time with each bit of, "Long dark hair, man's shirt, mid-twenties, tall."

Having to use a description instead of a name meant, it seemed to Apple, that Angus Watkin knew almost nothing; meant that the One-watcher had not made a connection with the Richway Hotel but had seen him only in the car—that last part was firm because Anna's colourful skirt had no part in the description.

"Ah, now I understand, sir," Apple said comfortably. "Of course, of course."

"Go on, Porter."

"That was a girl from whom I might get some chloroform."

You are a liar Angus Watkin's manner stated while he was saying, "I did tell you to call in for whatever was needed, you know, Porter."

"Yes, sir, but—"

The shriek came from right behind him. Recognizing it as laughter, after the first shocked second, didn't stop Apple from completing his shudder. Settling, he looked at the others. That Angus Watkin hadn't had the same reaction was only to be expected. That the two women were unaffected struck Apple as odd.

Which gave him the truth. The pair were, after all, here now as stage dressing, and had no connection with Upstairs. They were faceless ones, with the usable condition of being stone-deaf.

That explained their tinny voices, their lack of general response, and the fact of them keeping their eyes off the talkers' faces—so that there would be no lip-reading.

"You were saying, Porter?"

"Forgotten, sir," Apple said absently. He was thinking that an attack of deafness would be a valid reason for a musician to be unable to perform.

Angus Watkin said, "Never mind. But do allow me to impress upon you that when I said you could ask for anything you wanted, I meant precisely that."

"Yes, sir."

"Anything, Porter. Not excluding physical, intimate needs." He cleared his throat delicately.

Apple said a stupid, "I'm fine, thank you." He felt about twelve years old. "That girl I was seen with, I assure you it wasn't romance."

Playing deaf himself, Watkin said, "Possibly you are too diffident to ask. Thus the mission could be endangered by the interference of pressing, gross desires."

"Really, sir, I—"

"But we can take care of that, Porter."

Apple blinked. "I beg your pardon?"

While indicating the two women with his eyes, Angus Watkin said, "These ladies are at your disposal."

Apple blinked again. "Oh?"

"Accommodation has been arranged for nearby. The whole incident should take only a short time. Afterwards you would be free to concentrate."

Apple, who fancied the pair like malaria, wanted to say, "All right, sir, I confess. Last night I did go with a girl who wasn't connected with the mission. She was a prostitute." But he daren't risk having Watkin think he had lied. His position in this caper was unsteady enough as it was.

"Well, Porter?"

"You are quite right, sir, as always," Apple said with a shy loll of his head. "I have been somewhat distracted by primitive urges."

Angus Watkin showed satisfaction by a slight movement of his hairline. "Therefore you will accompany these ladies."

"Yes, sir," Apple said. "Thank you." He thought that he shouldn't have too much trouble in getting out of the situation, once away from his Control.

Snapping a look at his watch he said, "I also have the urge to get on with the mission."

"Finish your drink, Porter."

He obeyed like a good little faceless one, which added to his pique—that from his not being totally right about the presence of the two women, that from Watkin thinking his carnal taste ran to such scrubbers.

The last made Apple feel guilty and snobbish. In rising, he touched the shoulder on either side of him, and, as the painted faces glanced up, gave each a smiling nod.

Angus Watkin asked, "What about the chloroform?"

"I probably won't need it, sir, as it happens. If I do, I'll call in."

"Good. But otherwise don't bother about calls. Just come along to the house with your catch."

"Yes, sir. Good afternoon."

"Good hunting, Porter."

As Apple followed the two women through the crowd, he couldn't help but notice that they had excellent figures and elegant walks. He tutted at himself for that and went on to appraise the shapely legs clad in black nylon.

The moment we're outside, he thought with firm resolve, I'll get away. I'll say I haven't enough time for fun and games, or that my head aches, or that I've got a venereal complaint, or that I'm impotent, or that I've given it up for Lent.

In single file they reached the door, where they were held up by a crush of customers. The woman in front of Apple turned and looked up at him with a smile. She had beautiful teeth.

"In case you didn't catch our names," she said, "I'm Lilly and that's Marsha."

"Call me Jim," Apple said. He answered the smile while telling himself: no, absolutely not. Think Anna.

Lilly had read his lips. She returned, "I know it's not Jim

but that don't matter. We're not Lilly and Marsha either. Funny racket, ain't it?"

"I suppose it is."

The crowd cleared and they moved on. Outside, Apple, who was still behind, came to a halt and said, "Now just wait a minute, girls."

Unable to hear him, however, the two women were walking on ahead. He hurried after them, his eyes on the swaying hips, caught up and took an elbow in either hand. The women stopped and looked at him. There was, he saw, real prettiness under the paint.

It occurred to Apple that they would be sure to report to Angus Watkin if he failed to go through with his supposed desire. It was their duty to do so. What he needed to do therefore was give his explanation to them at length, and then ask for cooperation. Which would take time. It couldn't be done right here because Watkin might come out at any moment.

Lilly asked, "What is it, Jim?" She made rapid motions with both hands for the benefit of Marsha, who then said, "Hello, Jim."

"Hello," Apple said. "I was wondering how far it is to this place."

They both pointed at a doorway six feet away and said as one, "Here, dear."

"Okay. Let's go."

Again in single file they went through the doorway and immediately onto a narrow flight of stairs. Apple was in the rear. Going up, he had a splendid view of Lilly's legs. He thought Anna furiously.

They went along a passage and into a room. It was simply and old-fashionedly furnished, like the digs of a maiden lady who had retired from missionary labours. The upright chairs and a table were cowed by the presence of a huge double bed with brasswork at head and foot.

While Lilly closed and bolted the door, Marsha went to the end of the room, to its one large window. She began to draw the drapes across.

Placing a bentwood chair as far from the bed as he could get it, Apple sat down. *The point is,* he practised, *I'm in a terrible hurry.*

Marsha turned from the drawn curtains, which had only slightly reduced the brightness in the room. Staying there, smiling at Apple, she started to unbutton her blouse.

Lilly said, "I hope you like blondes, Jim." She was leaning against the door.

Apple looked at her quickly, to stop looking at Marsha. "Blondes?" His voice sounded like a cheap violin.

"That's what we are really. The brown at the roots is a dye. But nothing's ever what it seems in this racket, is it?"

Apple managed to come down the scale for another no-comment, "I suppose not."

"Still and all," Lilly said. "It is nice to be with someone on our own team. Makes a change."

Apple looked back at Marsha. She was slowly undoing her blouse's bottom button, her eyes still on Apple. He clenched his fists and blurted:

"I'm in a terrible hurry."

"Yes, dear," Marsha said, and pulling the button free she quickly slipped the blouse back off her shoulders.

"I didn't mean that," Apple said. "No."

Marsha nodded. "Good. I'm all for a bit of the slow titillation, me. It turns me on." Back to languid movements, she tossed the removed blouse aside. Her bra was frothy black lace and fit to bust.

Apple got up. He had decided to leave at once. But now he reminded himself that almost certainly the One-watcher would be outside and realize that he, Apple, hadn't been in the room long enough for frolic.

Sitting again, Apple watched Marsha unfasten and unzip

her skirt. When she began to ease it down, he switched his eyes to Lilly.

He told her, "Headache."

"What is, dear? The racket? I'll say it is. That there old Angus is a true blue bastard."

"Well . . ."

Lilly asked, "What d'you think of him yourself, Jim?"

Despite his twitching nerves, his divided concentration, his inability to think of the name he should be thinking, Apple was tempted to take this opportunity. He might not have the chance again to give an honest opinion on his Control. Never had he disliked Angus Watkin more than he did at this moment.

Apple, however, realized that the women could have been primed to try to get from him such an opinion. Watkin was capable of anything, even if the result hurt his personal vanity.

Apple rubbed his nose, thus covering his mouth, while he said, "Old Angus makes Machiavelli seem like Abraham Lincoln."

"What was that, dear?"

To ignore the question, Apple had to pretend strident interest in the other woman. He told himself.

Marsha stepped forward out of her skirt, which lay on the floor. She stood in a willowy pose, hands on rounded hips. She wore a black garter-belt to support the stockings that came so high they nearly touched the centre point of her sheer black briefs.

Apple stared plaintively. His Adam's apple made a slow trip up, a slow trip down. The sound of his gulp was clearly audible in the silent room. Apple was glad he was the only one who could hear it.

With a grace that any ballet dancer might have envied, Marsha sent her arms forward and around in a sort of aquatic breast-stroke movement. It finished when her hands were behind her back, up by the band of her bra.

Apple snapped his gaze to Lilly. Glaring, he said, "Listen, I have a complaint."

"Haven't we all, dear," Lilly said. "That old Angus isn't an easy man to work for."

"No, I mean a real one. A complaint, not a grumble. It's something I have to explain to you."

"I don't get you, dear," Lilly said cheerfully. "And anyway, why don't you finish getting undressed?" With the question she glanced at the floor near Apple's feet.

He bent forward, looked down. He was astounded to see that he had heeled off one shoe. Quickly stooping lower, he started fumblingly to put the shoe on again.

"Understand me, please," he said. "To put it bluntly, I have a disease." He waited. Hearing nothing, he realized that, with his head lowered, Lilly hadn't been able to see his lips.

Straightening, Apple said, "I have a disease which . . ."

Again Lilly hadn't seen to lip-read. Wearing an encouraging smile she was looking at Marsha. Apple did the same with his face straight.

Apple tried to look away. He didn't quite make it, but went on trying, his head giving short, abortive turns to one side like someone saying maybe.

Apple gave up trying to look away.

Lilly applauded quietly. Marsha, holding her pose, responded by waving her fingers as though ordering some bubbles to dance with.

Apple came to life. Muttering insanely that he was in a hurry to make a complaint about his headache which came from the impotence of working for someone whom he would give up for Lent any time, he bent to his feet.

Sadly and dazedly, Apple saw that he had heeled off his other shoe.

He went on gazing down until he heard movement. Raising his trunk, he saw that Marsha had come to the foot of the bed. She leaned on the brasswork, showing him a smile and her true blondness.

Lilly spoke. "Well, Jim," she said, "there's only one thing left to settle."

Apple played that violin again for a long, drawn-out, "Oh?"

Lilly asked, "Do you want me to go or stay? And if I stay, do you want me nude or dressed or a bit of each? And do you want me to join in or just watch? Or, in fact, do you want something special? Don't worry, we know how kinky the men are in this racket."

"Thank you," Apple said weakly, reaching up to unfasten his tie. "But I think that Marsha will be enough by herself. More than enough." He added after a pause, earnestly, "Please don't be offended."

Half an hour later, Apple emerged into the village square. His clothes were as neat as always, yet he felt sure he must be showing signs of raffishness. He was unaware that he had one eyebrow raised in a blasé lilt.

As he unlocked the car, however, Apple put the bout with Marsha out of his mind. It would be savoured later, at leisure. Now he had things to do.

Apple drove off, but slowed as soon as he was clear of Highgate and stopped at the first public telephone. He went in the kerbside booth.

With one foot holding the door open on account of his claustrophobia, Apple looked in the directory. He found the number of the Richway Hotel, dialled it after feeding the coin slot, and asked to be connected with Miss Schmidt.

The receptionist said, "Can't oblige, sir. Sorry. Miss Schmidt has left strict orders that she is not to be disturbed throughout today, by anyone."

So much for the idea of using deafness as an excuse, Apple thought. And it wasn't possible to send a telegram because they no longer existed in this country.

Apple began leafing again through the telephone directory. He whistled as a cover. Among the Js in one particular section of the yellow pages, he was surprised when his down-creeping finger came to rest at the name of Grinning Jim Jolly.

But, undismayed by the strange tricks of coincidence, Apple dialled the car lot. A recorded voice told him in a confidential manner, just between the two of them, that the office was closed until Monday.

Apple returned to the car and drove away.

Within minutes he was turning into a street of dismal terrace houses. Their doors opened directly to the pavement. In some windows, newsprint took the place of curtains. Cats prowled thinly. The street looked fit to live in for hours.

Apple parked and locked the Mazda, went to a mouldering door and rapped efficiently. Delving in his pocket he brought out a neatly folded wad of money. He hoped distantly that he still looked raffish.

The door opened. Ogden Renfrew, wearing a shabby bathrobe and a silk top hat, said a dramatic, "Lower the drawbridge for this travel-begrimed wayfarer."

"Hello, Og."

"Many's the weary furlong has he journeyed this day, as is bespoken by the care upon his dusty features."

"Here's your fee," Apple said, holding out the money. "It's the union rate."

Ogden Renfrew took the wad and dropped the drama. "Thanks, laddie. Come in. You are welcome to Elsinore and all that jazz."

Following along a dim passage, Apple asked, "What's

the hat all about? Breaking it in for a friend?" He laughed. He always laughed at his own jokes.

Coolly, the actor said, "I wear it when I'm reading Ibsen. One should, I believe."

They arrived in a living-room. It was a mess. Sole neat note came from the walls, which were covered with theatrical posters and photographs of the great stage names. None of the photographs were signed.

Apple asked, "Did you know that performances of Ibsen's *Ghosts* were banned for years in Britain?"

"No," Ogden Renfrew said shortly, turning. His manner had become severe. "But I'll tell you what I *do* know."

Taken aback by the older man's attitude, Apple paused in the act of reaching in his pocket for the false moustache. "Eh?"

"You, Appleton Porter, are in trouble."

"Trouble? What're you blathering about?"

"Blather nothing," Renfrew said. "You can't pull the wool over *my* eyes." He stepped forward and pushed Apple in the chest. "Sit down."

Apple did. He had to. Staggering back from the push, he hit his calves on the front of an armchair, into which he then fell. He fell deeply, legs lifting, for the springs of the seat were either lifeless or had been removed.

The actor said, "That's better."

Knees almost touching his chest, Apple gaped up. "What's wrong with you, for Christ's sake?"

"Nothing wrong with *me,* laddie. It's you. All that nonsense about Annas and Mavises and Judys, plus Rollses and Jags and Daimlers. You must think I'm an idiot."

"You're acting like one."

"Humph," Ogden Renfrew said. He turned aside and strode to the door, locked it and put the key in his pocket, during which action Apple tried to get up. He had nearly succeeded, legs waving and eyes tight, when the actor returned and sent him back into the hole with a light shove.

"Now you listen to me, Appleton Porter."

Settling, breathing heavily, Apple said a cold, "You look ridiculous with that hat on."

"You don't look exactly patrician yourself, folded up like a trussed chicken."

"All right, all right."

"Are you going to listen?"

"Looks as if I'll have to."

Ogden Renfrew folded his arms with a threat, like a teacher in kindergarten. He said, "Let's not bother to go into the absurd story you told me. Suffice it to say I know it was a load of rubbish. Okay?"

"No."

"Furthermore, I went back to the alley's end as soon as I realized I wasn't being followed. I peeked out. There was no girl. I saw you walking off in the distance and, closer, a couple of men. They were obvious criminal types."

"Og," Apple said patiently. "Girl or no girl, and types apart, what have two men being on that same street got to do with me?"

"For one thing—minor—they were watching you. For another thing—major—I heard in their mumble of talk the use of your sobriquet: Russet."

Apple winced, both at the mention of his hated nickname, which came from a type of apple and related to his penchant for blushing, and at the fact that the two operatives had used it.

"Aha," the actor said. "You realize, I see, that the game is up."

"You see nothing of the kind."

"Yes, yes, I stumbled upon the truth. It's all as clear as noon in Bombay."

"This is crazy," Apple said, struggling to rise. He had hardly got started before the actor pushed him with merely a contemptuous forefinger on the brow.

Ogden Renfrew resettled his top hat. He said, less severe, "You're in trouble, laddie. Patently you have got yourself mixed up in some kind of underworld activity."

"Nonsense."

"But never fear. I am your friend. And I, Apple, am going to help you."

"Og, I do not, repeat not, need any help. I am not mixed up in anything."

Renfrew nodded. "Yes, you are. I can sense it, apart from the evidence of absurd stories, impersonations by me and sinister-looking types. You're giving out different vibes from the usual."

"I'm in love."

"Maybe you are. And maybe she's a gangster's moll. All I want you to do is tell me about it. We'll put our heads together and perhaps enlist the help of a friend of mine at the local police station. He's almost a sergeant."

"I have nothing to say."

"The door is locked," Renfrew warned. "You don't leave here until you tell me all."

Apple would have smiled (at the insanity of the situation, out of fondness for the actor) except for realizing that Ogden Renfrew was quite capable of sticking to his threat. That made Apple think of the caper as ruined; think that Anna would cancel her concert and that Josef would look for a contact who never showed up.

"I'm waiting, Appleton Porter."

"If I could get out of this rotten chair. The position's making my belly ache."

"Sorry about that," Ogden Renfrew said. "But it all adds to the effect."

"You're a bloody sadist."

Smiling fatly: "True."

Apple was about to try again to extricate himself, using all his power, but held off on recalling how easily, one-fingeredly, Renfrew had pushed him down. He was double-trapped.

Apple put his head back, closed his eyes and thought about it. He reached the following conclusions:

He daren't risk giving another invented story, the actor being too perceptive—he had sensed Apple's mission-bred stimulation. Nor, of course, could the truth be told. Breaking a window (once free of the chair) was definitely out: such violence would convince Renfrew of underworld involvement and he might go to his almost-sergeant friend, causing all manner of unwanted complications. The only answer was to somehow get the key.

Apple raised his head, opened his eyes. "Og," he said, "you are totally mistaken about all this. It's a love triangle with no illegal goings-on."

"I don't believe you," the actor said. He had stepped back to the wall, was leaning elegantly on John Barrymore.

"It's true, and I have a date shortly with the lady I love. I have to be there. So please give me the key, Og."

"Shan't."

"At least let me get up."

"Absolutely not. You might get rough."

Taking his gaze on a slow wander around the room, Apple found himself starting to feel seriously worried. Feebly he asked, "May I smoke, please?"

"Okay. But don't try any tricks."

With difficulty, Apple first reached and then dug into a pocket. He paused, smiling.

"That's more like it," the actor said. "Now spill every bean."

Slowly, his smile taking on an evil cast, Apple drew from one pocket his cigarette lighter, from another a V-shaped bunch of white hairs. The latter he held up delicately between finger and thumb.

Staring, Ogden Renfrew leaned away from the wall. He said, "Why, that's my . . ."

"It is," Apple said. He flicked on the cigarette lighter and moved it close to the false moustache. "I'll burn it to a cinder if you don't give me the key."

The actor had paled. "You wouldn't dare."

"Og, I love this lady. She means much more to me than your tash. The key, if you please."

"No. I refuse."

"Okay," Apple said, shrugging. "Be it on your own head. Here goes." He moved the flame underneath the moustache.

Ogden Renfrew flung his hands out and shouted, "No, stop, I give in, I give in."

Three minutes later Apple was getting in the Mazda. His feeling of power and cleverness had been dispelled by the actor saying, quietly, as he unlocked the door, "I was only trying to help you."

But Apple cheered up on reminding himself, again, how well he was doing on this operation.

Presently, driving at an idle, Apple asked himself what he could do now. There were two or three hours to kill before he went home to prepare for the next stage. He wondered what the pros did when they had time on their hands.

They went to sophisticated, dimly lit dives, Apple supposed, where they were on intimate terms with the owner, whatever the city, whichever the country, and where they drank fingers of Scotch, laughed harshly, and allowed sultry-looking women to light their cigarettes.

In the West End half an hour later, after parking in a garage, Apple went to the movies.

At home, while eating a snack of cold sausages with the grease scraped off, Apple tried E.S.P. That, parapsychology, had been the theme of the film he had seen, but no more than that could he recall, having spent most of his time in the cinema directing two-reel daydreams. They all featured Anna and himself, the screenplays had been unconsciously plagiarized from Marsha, and the location was Ethel's back seat.

With each mouthful of sausage, Apple closed his eyes and thought, *Deaf, deaf, deaf*. However, the noise in his head from eating ran a strong interference.

He tried again when the sausages were finished. But the repeated word became meaningless. Worse, it began to seem oppressive. Feeling vaguely threatened, Apple gave up on extra-sensory perception and left the whole business in the hands of chance.

After a bed-sprawl to digest his snack, Apple started to change into running gear. Monico, wandering in to investigate the sounds of activity, went into his usual cavort of excitement on seeing the track suit.

Where another dog would have barked, Monico gasped heavily while leaping and twirling. He had a singular lack of grace. Twice he tripped himself up.

Changed, Apple went to the apartment door, which he opened and stood wide. He nodded a caution down at Monico, who had calmed from wild anticipation to a near-catatonic state of containment. He trembled rigidly.

Apple leaned out and looked both ways. The scene was clean. He went out and strolled along the passage, humming a German beer hall song.

Apple passed the door of 3B, through which came soft

radio music, reached the stairwell corner and started to go down in a loose-limbed trot.

On the landing below, Apple changed step in time with his hum. He turned onto the next flight of stairs and at its midway point hopped over the step that squeaked.

Taking the final flight, Apple came into the entrance hall. All was satisfyingly quiet, including the corridor that passed the landlord's flat.

Apple circled the centre table and went to the front door. After working his way through a luxurious yawn, he freed the lock, turned a handle and began to draw the door open.

With a breath-catch of startlement that hurt the back of his throat, Apple froze when he had the wood six inches from its frame.

On the step outside, near enough to reach out and touch, standing shoulder to shoulder, were Flaco and Gordo.

The two men looked to be as startled as Apple by the sudden confrontation. For seconds on end they stared at him while he stared at them.

Next, all was action.

Apple, with a rush, tried to close the door. Flaco and Gordo, acting as one, swept their arms up against it and pushed. The contest was brief: two into one will go.

Apple was thrust away as the door came open. He careened backwards. The backs of his upper thighs hit the table. Impetus carried him over and onto his back. He slid across the polished surface to the farther end—and his shoulders went out into space.

Twisting mightily, Apple turned a semi-somersault. It took him sideways off the table. With a loud crash he landed on his hands and knees. The noise followed a louder one, from the door bashing against the wall.

Apple leapt up. Flaco and Gordo were on the table's

other side. With a yard of space between them, they stood in forward leans, their hands out like lying anglers. Under their hat brims their eyes glinted malevolently.

Apple also saw, from the edge of his vision, a spectator. The early-teens schoolgirl was watching with interest through the gaping doorway.

Yet Apple was unaware of being a show-off as he fell into the official crouch of unarmed combat and began to circle the table. Forming his hands into slices, he hoped he would be able to remember the details from Training Two.

After nodding heavily, as though by way of introduction, the fat man of the pair spoke, snapping, "We want to talk to you."

"No burglars allowed in here," Apple growled. "It's a rule of the house."

Thin Flaco said, "We're not burglars. Which you know well and good."

They both had standard British accents, Apple noted. He said glibly, "I don't know a thing."

With himself and partner backing away at a creep, Gordo said, "If you try any rough stuff, you'll be sorry."

Flaco: "Yes, you will. I promise you."

"Promises, promises," Apple said. He found that a little disappointing. "Get out."

Gordo: "After we've had a talk."

"Nothing to talk about," Apple snarled, throwing a fast glance at the doorway, the schoolgirl, to see how he was doing. He seemed to be doing fine, judging from her expression of awe.

"That's what you think, chum," Flaco sneered.

Gordo added, "If you can think at all."

"Are you two clowns leaving or not?"

They shook their heads.

Taking a deep breath like someone getting ready for a

joke's punch line, Apple gave a samurai yell. It came off well. In fact it came off so well, rose so loud, that Apple was unnerved himself.

Thus his attack lacked verve and precision.

His two judo chops at Gordo met only air. The fat man had better luck, or skill. His straight John L. Sullivan left landed solidly in the middle of Apple's chest, sending him into a reverse skitter.

Recovering, Apple shot an abashed look at the doorway. He was relieved to see that the schoolgirl had gone—chased, he felt sure, by his impressive yell. But he decided not to try another one.

"If you take it easy," Flaco said, "you'll be okay."

Apple said, "Go biblical-sense yourself."

"Well, you asked for it, chum."

Gordo: "Here goes."

Side by side like bacon and egg, the unmatched pair began to come forward. As they did, Flaco released a long, strident hiss of impending battle.

The sharp sound echoed around the hallway and wafted up the stairwell.

Apple retreated, the while smiling grimly as if he knew what he was doing. Flaco's hiss having faded, there was silence. It was broken by a noise from above: a drumming and scrambling.

Flaco and Gordo stopped. Apple stopped. The noise grew rapidly louder.

As Apple glanced behind him at the staircase, Monico appeared there. Tongue waving like hello, he kept his balance from the turn and came on down. He flailed his long-legged way off the bottom step and went into a skid on the floor.

Apple leapt aside. He grabbed his dog by the collar just as Monico seemed to be on the point of falling over, looked at the men and snarled:

"This is your last chance to leave."

They both said, "What?"

Releasing Monico, Apple stood erect and thrust out a pointing arm. He shouted, "Kill!"

Flaco and Gordo snapped to bustling life. They raced the short distance to the door and crashed together in getting outside, where they disappeared along the street.

Apple sagged, letting his tension go. He looked down. Monico gazed up at him happily, tail on the wag.

A voice from behind asked, "What's all this?"

Apple straightened as he turned, clicked back to tension when he saw the landlord.

Charles Lampton stood at the mouth of the back corridor, hunched with satisfied disbelief inside the green tweed suit that was dying of exhaustion. He was staring at Monico.

"What," he repeated, "is all this?"

Apple tried at speed to think of an out. One wouldn't come even slowly. He fumbled a foolish, unpremeditated, "Sorry the noise disturbed you."

"Noise?" the landlord said absently. His right arm was now extended toward Monico. "I can't hear a thing when my door's closed."

Not wanting to know that, Apple ignored the information. In any case, he was edging towards an out. Doing a poor imitation of a smile he said:

"Well, well, aren't you the sly one, though."

"I beg your pardon?"

"All this time, Mr. Lampton, despite the no-pets rule, you've had a dog."

The landlord looked up. "*I've* had a dog?"

"Cunning old you. I found it here when I came downstairs. Two seconds ago. What's its name?"

"I don't know, Mr. Porter. It's not my dog."

"Does it eat a lot?"

"It is not, Mr. Porter, my dog."

"It's not your dog?" Apple asked, switching to a feeble impersonation of astonishment.

"It is definitely not my dog."

"Then whose dog is it?"

Charles Lampton's arm had sagged. He said, "Don't you know whose dog it is, Mr. Porter?"

"No, Mr. Lampton. I never saw this dog before, ever. Does it bite?"

"It isn't my dog, Mr. Porter."

They looked at one another gravely. Apple asked, "Could it belong to one of the residents?"

"That, Mr. Porter, is entirely possible."

Apple, after glancing around the hall, finishing with its front, put on a dud copy of understanding. "But of course," he said. "How slow of me not to have realized it before."

"What, Mr. Porter?"

"The door, Mr. Lampton."

"What about it?"

"Well, it's open."

"So I see."

"It was like that when I came downstairs," Apple said. "One second ago. Somebody must have forgotten to close it. That does happen sometimes. And the dog, ugly brute that it is, obviously came in to look for food."

Again absently, Charles Lampton said, "It is on the thin side." He added, less absently, "Also, it's tall."

Apple lifted fast, sagged hands in a bad act of surprise while gazing down. "Why, I do believe that is a name-plate on the collar."

"Where? Wait—I'll get my glasses."

"That's all right," Apple said, stooping to play a look at

the bare leather. "I have it. Ah yes. I know that street. I shall take the brute around there at once." He chuckled like an emptying bottle. "Maybe I'll get a reward."

With Charles Lampton saying for him to wait a minute and asking what street was it, Apple went by him while calling out various dog-type names and saying he would go the back way because it was quicker. Monico followed.

Minutes later they were free and running, both as bouncily gleeful as truants.

Apple was easy about the incident with Charles Lampton, apart from a barely acknowledged feeling that fate should somehow have arranged for it to have happened when things were slow and he needed it.

As for Flaco and Gordo, the only point Apple had learned from the encounter was that the pair had no deep training in unarmed combat, which meant that they were probably not associated with any espionage organization. Which really didn't tell him much.

Apple and Monico ran for two hours. Back at Harlequin Mansions they successfully gained an unseen entry. Apple fed his dog and gave him an extra measure by way of a medal for his bravery earlier downstairs.

Stripping off the track suit, Apple showered. Afterwards he put on his tuxedo—without enthusiasm.

As is known to the world's overweight, black slims its wearer; not for nothing is that simple little black dress so common. In Apple's case, appearing thinner made him look taller. But he had to dress formally for the two events, the theatre and the late supper. He compensated by checking his image nowhere except in the kitchen mirror, which showed him only from the chest up.

Apple left the flat and went down to the hall. The last delivery of mail having arrived, letters were lined up neatly on the table.

Apple picked up one addressed to himself. He would

have opened it but for hearing landlord sounds from the passage. Another talk with Lampton he didn't need at the moment.

Slipping the letter into his pocket, Apple left the house. He headed for the nearby basement garage. During the walk he kept a wary eye out for Flaco and Gordo, as well as being attentive to his back in case it recorded the trailing finger.

While he was driving south and crossing the river to the Royal Festival Hall, Apple found tension growing in him gradually. It was a feeling of suspense which he could enjoy, for he had almost nothing to lose, a great deal to gain.

By the time he had parked the Mazda, however, squeezed in among countless other cars, Apple was thinking gain exclusively. And by the time he had got out of the car he was seeing the future as it would be if Anna cancelled her concert and Josef agreed to defect.

Oblivious to the vehicular bustle around him, Apple conjured up visions of himself as a successful espionage agent, a three-star pro, a top operative to whom Upstairs was so familiar that he often yawned there, and sometimes gazed around with a poignant smile for the innocent he had once been.

He saw young agents hanging on his every word, copying his style, wearing lifts in their shoes to make themselves taller. He saw himself strolling the boulevards of foreign capitals. He saw a wardrobe full of trench coats. He saw pretty secretaries gasp when he rested a nonchalant hand on their shoulders. He saw men in clubland whispering, "You know who that is, don't you?"

One scene Apple enjoyed so much that he ran it again. In it he was handing a gold watch to a subdued Angus Watkin, who was retiring from the service.

Apple came alert to find that he was still standing beside

his car. He locked it and strode towards the Royal Festival Hall.

The huge, flower-garbed foyer was crowded. Most men were in black tie, most women wore evening dresses. At the sides, people were moving, funnelling into the doors to the auditorium. The centre patch was held by the stationary: those members of the music world who needed to be seen by other members, and the outsiders who hoped to pass as members by the fact of association.

It lacked ten minutes to curtain-up.

Apple joined the movers, whereas normally at concerts he lingered on the sidelines to pick out the celebrated and to wish he were bold enough to join the inner outsiders.

His knees in a sag out of unconscious habit, Apple came to a door. The girl who glanced at his ticket reminded him of Marsha. He cleared his throat and told himself that there was actually no resemblance.

The girl said, "Number nine on the front row, sir."

"Thank you very much," Apple said, and was not aware of looking the girl straight in the face while he mouthed the words elaborately.

Passing on, he made his way to the front row, to the costly seat he had bought when he had known Anna Schmidt only through reputation and photographs, and would have scoffed at the prophecy that within days he would become on close terms with her.

After sitting, Apple shuffled low, another unconscious habit. It had been sired by a thousand cruel remarks heard from behind him in theatres.

Apple looked at his watch. It showed four minutes to go. He twisted glances behind in both directions. The auditorium was mostly filled, with only a few people still finding their seats.

Until the four minutes had passed, Apple checked with

his watch some twenty-odd times. The suspense which had him in its grab had stopped being enjoyable. He was on edge, nervous, as taut as an archer's neck.

Between checks on the time, Apple had stared at the curtain in front of him. He went on doing so now and felt a slight easing in his tension as it stayed still and closed.

The audience, which had quietened as curtain-up time had neared, began to reverse that procedure. The rustling became a clattering, the whispering became a drone.

Apple looked at his watch at last. The concert was six minutes late in starting.

After shaking his forearm and listening to his watch, Apple leaned towards the man beside him. "Excuse me," he said. "Do you have the precise time, please?"

The man nodded dully, as cold as cowards' feet. With a slowness that made Apple almost give up and ask the person on his other side, he brought out a pocket watch, which he tapped twice before opening.

He turned the face towards Apple while saying, "Seven minutes and forty-five seconds after."

"Thank you," Apple said. "It looks as though there's a hold-up."

The man put his watch away with a sigh. "No public performance anywhere in the world can be guaranteed to start on time, except the bullfight in Spain."

That was no help. Apple straightened. He stared on at the curtain, glancing at his watch, listening to the gradual rise in audience noise and wondering if he should mention to the man that, curiously enough, the word "bullfight" didn't exist in Spanish.

Apple stiffened. There had been a ripple in the curtain. Now, the ripple appeared again and moved along into the middle. The audience noise quickly ran down.

The curtain split long enough to allow a man to come

through. He was stout, distinguished-looking and held a piece of paper in one hand.

He wore an expression of apology.

In Apple, hope soared.

Dry-washing one wrist, the man said, "Ladies and gentlemen, I'm sorry to report that there has been an accident."

The audience rumbled and hissed. Apple sat tight.

"Which accident," the man said, "has necessitated a change in arrangements."

Apple smiled. He could feel the gold watch in his hand, hear Angus Watkin's halting, pathetic speech of farewell.

"As you know," the man on-stage said, "the introduction was to have been made by the chairman of the British Music Society. Unfortunately, however, Sir Ralph was involved in a car accident on his way here tonight. Although unhurt physically, he has a slight case of shock and has been taken home. I, therefore, shall try to fill Sir Ralph's able shoes, and myself introduce our recitalist."

The audience calmed. Apple slumped.

He didn't hear the following laudatory remarks. Nor did he get the expected thrill when, the man bowing and leaving, the curtains swept back.

Anna Schmidt was revealed. She was alone on the vast stage, which had a background of potted palms. Wearing a long white dress, Anna stood in a modest pose beside a grand piano.

The audience was clapping. With the exception of Apple, who sat on in his slump of dejection, everyone applauded vigorously. The sound grew. As it did, people began to stand. Soon, everybody was on his feet, again with the exception of one person.

Solemn at the standing acclaim, more common after a performance than before, Anna moved away from the piano and came to the footlights. She bowed deeply. On straightening, she noticed Apple, lone sitter.

At the same time, Apple recalled everything that this young girl had fought against and accomplished. Slowly he rose. He started to clap.

Holding Anna's eyes, Apple smiled as he clapped; smiled and nodded; signalled respect, fondness and encouragement; told her by his manner that he not only understood why she was going ahead with the performance, but also approved.

Anna smiled. Shifting her attention to the audience in general, she spread her arms, bowed again and gave all the usual gestures of thanks plus requests for the ovation to come to an end.

It did. The clapping ran its course, the people started to return to their seats. Apple was the last to stop applauding, last to sit down.

Anna stayed where she was, at the footlights. When the audience had finally settled, she spoke. Head raised, voice clear, she said:

"Thank you so very much, ladies and gentlemen, for that wonderful reception. It thrilled and moved me. You have made me feel both humble and proud."

Anna took a step forward. "I should like to show my appreciation of your response by playing for you, before the recital proper, a special piece of music."

The audience murmured. Anna, after a quick glance at Apple, went on, "I wrote the piece myself, and its title is the 'Cancellation Waltz.'"

That would do it, Apple thought excitedly. It couldn't help but do it. The title was a clear indication. The rest was up to Josef.

Apple sat taut and happy and fretful in his seat on the front row. Anna was playing the first of her scheduled pieces, having finished the waltz, which owed more to Chopin than Schmidt. Apple wanted to leave, but felt that he ought to wait for a better moment.

Calm, he cautioned himself even while wondering chafingly: what if Josef, watching the telecast during a snatched minute from the banquet, had missed the start and seen only this, the playing? And what if he had seen Anna speaking but hadn't had anyone there with him to translate what she had said, the title of her waltz?

Apple was familiar with the piece being played by Anna. It, he reckoned, was at least ten minutes away from completion. He felt that he couldn't and shouldn't wait that long.

Now, he told himself. Leave now.

But the audience sat rapt. There wasn't a sound or movement in the house, except for those from the girl at the piano keyboard, and even her playing in this passage was languid. Apple had a horror of unconsciously starting to fidget. He clenched his every muscle.

Sweating, Apple sat it out.

As soon as the piece ended and the audience burst into applause, he left his seat in a crouch, the while managing to throw a glance at Anna. She gave the faintest of nods.

Saggy with relief, Apple left the auditorium by a side-door. Within minutes he was folding his long body into the car. It took him longer to extricate the Mazda from between the siding pair of cars, longer still to get out of the maze of lanes that criss-crossed the parked vehicles. Once finally getting to the road, he had become hotly tense again.

Apple drove swiftly. It was an easement now, not a nuisance, having to sit hunched over the steering-wheel because of limited headroom. The position made him feel that he was going faster.

Apple didn't believe it when he came up behind a police

patrol car. Its driver was proceeding at the proper thirty miles an hour. To Apple it seemed like ten.

The road was a railed-in throughway, with limited exits and entries. Peering ahead, around the police car, Apple could see no signs of the traffic lights that would announce the location of an escape-way. He groaned and swayed like the victim he felt.

Apple weighed the pros and cons. If he stayed behind, it could put another quarter of an hour on the trip across to the hotel in Hammersmith; if he passed the police, and if they stopped him for speeding, it could delay him fatally—now being a slack time of evening, before the drunks came out to sway, the officers would take their unsweet time about examining papers and writing out a summons.

Although he had not actually made a decision, con or pro, Apple found himself changing into second gear. He steered out to the crown of the road and roared ahead. He flashed his lights, he blasted his horn.

The pair of uniformed men twisted around. The driver pulled closer to the kerb.

Apple drew level. One-handed he made wild signals, at the same time cavorting his features and rocking his head. He had no idea what the men would make of it all.

Nothing, apparently, for they merely gaped. The next second, Apple was past. He cut over and roared on and waited to see what would happen.

Hitting sixty, he changed down and told himself that, if the police gave chase, he could always dump the Mazda, escape on foot and get a cab.

But the patrol car stayed behind and in its legal crawl. Apple concluded that he had been taken for a colleague, and that he had therefore pulled off quite a coup. It was a fine omen. Nothing could stop him now.

Driving illegally, but not insanely, Apple soon came into Hammersmith. He realized that he didn't know how to get to the hotel, the Forge. Stopping, he leaned out of the window and asked a passer-by, who kept on passing.

The next two people also ignored the query, quickening their steps. The fourth person, with beard and turban, gave directions in fractured English.

After puzzling out a series of one-way streets, Apple located the hotel. It was new and starkly attractive. On the forecourt stood an airline coach, around which milled a crowd: fans and the curious, and one man with a placard asking that Poland not be forgotten.

Driving past, Apple managed to find a parking slot nearby. He walked back smartly and halted at the edge of the crowd. The first person his eyes settled on, in looking around for a likely someone to ask about the banquet's progress, was the man with the ski-jump nose. Gateman saw Apple at the same moment.

Just briefly did that questioning expression touch the Hammer's face. Recognition came next. Apple could only suppose that he had been seen going by in the car, which Gateman was bound to remember.

Apple ducked into the crowd, legs bent. Near the coach he looked back with a quick bob up. Gateman was following. Behind him came a priest and a man in postman uniform.

Slipping around the front of the bus, Apple reached its door. He went inside and did a Groucho Marx along the aisle. The rear emergency door was closed. Apple opened it and stepped outside.

Near the far end he could see Gateman and the disguised Hammers craning up to see over heads. Apple went the other way. That brought him to the hotel entrance. With a shrug of play-it-by-development, he went in.

The lobby was supposed to represent a blacksmith's shop in a bygone era. It had mock-stone walls, ceiling beams made of plastic and a forge that gave off a real-looking glow. The desk was in the shape of a horseshoe.

Hanging around the sides were signs, their words burned into slabs of natural wood. Apple chose the one that said BANQUETING HALL, went under it and along a passage.

Through an archway he came into a large dining-room. He halted among a group of people who were standing by the threshold and who, to his surprise, glanced at him without interest instead of giving him the begone-interloper glare.

Apple realized why. He, like the score of waiters who were moving around the one long table, was dressed in a black-tie outfit. He was assumed to be one of the staff.

In a far corner of his mind, Apple registered that it was sharp of him to have put on his tuxedo.

The hundred-odd people at the table were in everyday clothes out of respect for the visitors. Russians never show the sartorial flag.

In a droop, Apple moved farther into the room. From a sideboard he picked up a plate and a napkin. The latter he draped over his forearm because that's what waiters did in the movies.

Apple walked along beside the banqueting table. He saw Josef. The folk singer, in the centre at the far side, was seated between two obvious Englishwomen.

Apple now spotted Josef's colleagues. Sitting together at the end for which Apple was headed, they were watching the new waiter with care.

Apple turned and went the other way. Circling, he arrived behind Josef's chair. He bent low, waiting for a break in the conversation which the singer was struggling to have with the woman on his right.

When the pause came, Apple leaned forward to the old man's left and whispered, in Russian, "Good evening, Josef."

Turning his head slightly to that side, the folk singer murmured, "Hello again, Jim."

"Did you see the telecast?"

"The opening, yes."

"Did you understand what Anna Schmidt said?"

Josef's head twitched a negative. "No, of course not."

"Oh."

"But someone told me. The 'Cancellation Waltz.' Very neat."

Apple said, "Yes, Josef, neat and real. It was meant for you, obviously."

"Obviously."

"She couldn't back out of the performance, so we thought up that angle for you. You must believe that."

"Oh, I do," the old man said. "I think it's wonderfully neat how you arranged it without disappointing hundreds of people, to mention nothing of the vast television audience. I do believe in you now."

Excitedly, Apple asked, "When does the banquet end?"

"It already has. The speeches are over. Everyone's just about to leave."

"Then you and I should slip away at once."

People around the table were beginning to stand. Josef himself got up. He turned. Smiling, he said, "You really are naive, Jim."

Apple, who had also risen, felt a gap in his excitement. "I am?"

"Absolutely. Did you actually believe that I would defect? That I would leave all that's dear to me? That I would turn my back on fame and fortune in exchange for an uncertain future in a strange land?"

"Well, I thought . . ."

"Of course you did," the old man said with a rogue twinkle in his eye and a japer's grin. "And I thank you."

"Thank me?"

"Yes, Jim. That little business with you was the most amusing thing that happened to me in Britain. I shall always remember it with pleasure."

Shaking his head, Apple asked, "You don't want to stay in the West?"

"Of course not."

Apple blinked slowly, like someone cleaning his eyes. He could think of nothing else to say. His excitement had gone. He stood on vacantly as Josef turned away to hand one of the Englishwomen out of her chair; stood on until he got a sense-warning of approach.

He glanced to either side.

On his left, the three other folk singers were coming, one behind the other. On his right, Gateman was leading the phony priest and imitation postman. All six had faces of cold determination.

Apple's hesitation was curt. He stepped past Josef, put down plate and napkin among the post-meal clutter and dropped quickly to his hands and knees.

He crawled under the table.

It was dim down there, like a basement with cobwebby windows, which suited the way Apple was feeling now that his emptiness was beginning to fade.

But he had to put his emotions on one side for the time being, in order to think clearly about a trouble-free exit. It would never do to compound failure with fiasco.

Not looking at a seated woman's legs, after the first look, Apple crawled to the other side of the table. There, at that point, he was blocked from getting out by chairs and standing people.

About to go on, head for a place farther along, he changed his mind when he got a better idea. It was born of the trade adage relating to the unexpected. He swung around with an awkward shuffle of limbs and went all-foursing back to the point of entry.

Emerging from under the table, Apple straightened his body while keeping on his knees.

Looking down at him were Josef and one of his dinner companions. The folk singer appeared to be amused, the woman worried. She asked aside in her atrocious Russian, "Is it a reporter?"

Apple didn't catch the answer. He was busy scanning for the enemy. He saw them. The three old men were on this side of the table farther down, stooping to look underneath. The trio of Hammers were on the other side, having just rounded the end. Both groups were between Apple and the exit arch.

He got up, slipped around the grinning Josef and went the other way. He had to twist and weave to get through the throng of staff and guests.

Ahead were two doors, Apple's height allowed him to see. Of the swing variety, they were the kitchen's IN and OUT and clearly marked so. In making for them, Apple glanced back.

He had been seen by the enemy. Which, he thought, was the old, old story in respect of his six feet, seven inches—one benefit for every ten instances of disadvantage.

Both Russian camps, the old and the young, were heading this way, though hindered by the crowd. Leading by a long stretch was the ersatz priest.

Apple forged on. He was beaten to the IN door by a waiter with a tray of dishes. The man's kick opened the way. Once through, he called out raucously, "Two black coffees!"

With the door swinging closed behind him, Apple shouted, "Fish and chips!"

Neither voice made much impression. The kitchen was a panic of noise and action and steam. Apple found the scene slightly intimidating, a baby hell.

He swung away to the side and went to the OUT door.

Going through, he came within feet of being face to face with the Hammer cleric. He made another fast turn and went through IN.

Unable to think of a food order, Apple shouted, "Hold the front page!"

He strode on into the panic. Seeing with a glance back that the Hammer had come in and was close behind, he circled a table that held a mound of poultry. He quickened his stride to pass a tall-hatted chef, whom he then pushed back to create a collision with the fake priest.

Apple went to the IN door. He crashed through. While relieved at not meeting a dish-laden waiter, he at the same time felt a twinge of disappointment.

On one side of the table, the three old men were nearing; at the other, Gateman and colleague. Apple went on and with one huge lift of his long legs strode up onto the table top at its end.

Calmly, as though this was something that happened here all the time, Apple walked along on the white tablecloth. He picked his way nonchalantly among the various articles, which rattled at his tread.

All the enemy Russians, having turned, were struggling to get through the crowd; it had become immobile, watching the table walker. The man with the ski-jump nose made no attempts at politeness as he shoved and pushed.

Apple scattered a tinkle of cutlery. After closely missing a cruet, he knocked over two bottles of relish, which made him feel like a dunce any teacher would have scolded. To aid precision, he put his tongue out at the corner of his mouth.

The folk singers were making headway, but Gateman was in the affronted clutch of a diner he had shoved.

With no more mishaps, Apple came to the end of the table. He remembered to retract his tongue before jumping to the floor. At a swift dart he went through the people, ignored a headwaiter who tried to stop him, went under the archway and along the passage, through the lobby and outside.

After rounding the coach, Apple stopped. The stimulation of the chase died away in him. His depression came back.

Apple knew there was no point in waiting, in hoping that jester Josef would have a last-minute change of mind. The mission was over. Over and lost.

Drably, Apple headed for his car.

Trouble was, Apple thought, as he idled along in the direction of Notting Hill, everything had looked so good, so golden, so indicative of success.

He *had* made a solid contact with one of the folk singers. He *had* managed not only to actually get to meet the famous Anna Schmidt, but to arrange through her a sort of proof of good intentions—quite an accomplishment in itself, that.

So it was only natural that he should feel low. Natural but wrong, stupid, because at the start of the caper failure had been expected and accepted.

Apple told himself that he ought, therefore, to cheer up. Yet he continued glum. There were so many clever things he had done that nobody would ever know about. Not Angus Watkin. Not his dossier.

Apple sighed heavily.

He tried for cheerfulness with the reminder that in a couple of hours he would be seeing Anna again. This was just beginning to work, the severity going out of his features, when he noticed the lights.

Meaning he registered after turning a corner that the headlights were still present. They had been behind him almost since he had left the hotel.

Apple knew, of course, that he could be mistaken about

having a tail. Not only that, but if he did have one, it couldn't be anything that would do him any good, caperwise.

In fact, Apple thought with his drabness back in full, it was probably the law: if not the original patrol car which he had raced past on the throughway, then another whose officers had picked up the radio message to be on the lookout for a tall, reckless and possibly insane driver in a red Mazda.

Apple was tempted to feed his despondency by allowing himself to get caught, snapped at and given a ticket, if not outright arrested. It would serve him right for getting big ideas about an impossible mission.

It was only the thought of somehow being prevented from attending Anna's post-recital supper that made Apple come out of his indifference.

He speeded up. At the first junction he came to he turned into a quiet street, where he gave the car still more power. Seconds later, the headlights appeared.

They were definitely the same pair: the nearside light had a yellowish tinge. The vehicle itself was unseeable behind the glare, even as a formless shape.

Apple slowed. So did the lights. Apple gunned his motor and sped ahead. After an initial loss of ground, the glare behind closed the gap.

To find out for certain whether or not the car was on his trail or merely being taken on an aimless wander, its driver following whatever appeared ahead, Apple cut off into more back streets. He also went along two alleys. The vehicle with jaundice in one eye stayed with him.

It was not without aim.

Apple twitched as he felt and heard a thudding. It came from below and had a drear familiarity. So what did he do, he wondered, if this meant a puncture?—quite apart from the fact that he had neglected to get the spare repaired.

But then Apple saw, on looking closely down at the road, that it was surfaced with old-fashioned cobblestones. His tyres were sound.

Apple rounded a corner to leave the cobbles behind. In his rear-view mirror the tail car appeared. He decided that the time had come to lose it.

For that he could use several routines out of Training Four. He settled on the one he fancied most.

The while looking around carefully for the right situation, Apple circled several blocks of residential streets. Finally he saw the usable, dark, open gateway near a corner and made his last circuit.

On turning the same corner again, having speeded up, he swung into the tree-canopied gateway, halted fast and killed the lights, but left his motor running. He remembered to use the hand-brake, keeping his foot off the brake pedal which would activate lights at the rear.

Via his rear-view he saw a flash and blur as the chase car went racing past. He counted five beats before reversing out at a cautious pace. The road was empty. Not until he had gone back around the corner did he put on his lights.

Apple had been uplifted by the action, especially by having had the opportunity to pull that disappearance routine at long last.

But as he drove on, and the streets in his mirror stayed clean of the chase car, Apple sank again to glum lethargy. He thought plaintively of gold watches.

Already in Notting Hill, Apple drove straight to Pater Road. He parked outside number eighteen, opposite the gate and the twin lines of stunted trees.

Unfolding himself out of his car, he locked up and went along the garden path. He gave the bell a short, dispirited ring. Almost at once the door opened.

Albert stood there with his skeletal face and fluffy grey

hair, mechanic's coveralls and running shoes of dubious white. Peering around Apple he asked:

"Are we alone?"

"I am."

"What's the weather like up there?"

Instead of telling the older man he had used that line before, Apple said tiredly, "Fine."

"Don't like your haircut."

"All right."

"Come in," Albert said, his tone implying surrender. "The door at the end. You're expected."

Uncannily, everything looked the same as on his first visit here. It was like a photograph that he had seen before: either one snapped by an amateur simply to use up the last of a roll of film, or one lovingly taken by a professional to capture the essence of suburban tedium.

Lights bleakly on, curtains drawn, fire feebling, the study with its minimum proportions formed a perfect setting for the man who sat at his seeming ease in a high-back armchair. No actor could have bettered Angus Watkin at portraying the ageing minor executive who, in his mortgaged home, pretends he knows nothing of quiet desperation.

Apple reached back and closed the door behind him. "Good evening, sir."

"Good evening, Porter," Angus Watkin said in his plain brown voice. "One trusts one is not detaining you from some formal frivolity."

Apple patted a silk lapel. "No, sir. I've been to a piano recital."

"Curious time for culture, Porter."

"It was business, sir, not pleasure."

Angus Watkin almost raised an eyebrow. "Connected, in fine, with the mission?"

"Precisely, sir."

"Which mission, I take it, as you appear to be alone, has not been brought to a successful conclusion."

"It has not, sir, no," Apple said, stopping himself at the last minute from hanging his head.

Angus Watkin raised his arm languidly in the direction of the matching armchair. He might have been pointing out a disappointing view. He said, "Sit down, Porter."

Obeying, Apple wondered of a sudden, without enthusiasm, if he should tell some sort of elaborate lie about near success at kidnapping one of the old folk singers. He realized, however, that he was too low in spirit. His powers of invention, not overly strong at the best of times, would be incapable of rising to the task.

Apple offered instead a dull, "The mission was far more complex than I had anticipated, sir."

Gingerly, Angus Watkin put his fingertips together. "On that score," he said, "I feel that I ought to apprise you of a certain fact."

"Yes, sir?"

"There has been the usual lack of liaison between departments. I hope you were not too inconvenienced."

Apple shook his head. "I don't understand, sir."

"The Special Branch," Watkin said. His tone was the one he reserved for all things dim and blemished, all creatures gross and mean. It was like a star referring to a stand-in.

Apple asked, "Scotland Yard's undercover people were trying to do the same thing I was, sir?"

"No, Porter. Certainly not. The Branch doesn't dabble in affairs of such subtlety. In any case, liaison is never quite as bad as that."

"No, sir."

"The matter was not connected with the mission. It had to do with a vehicle."

Apple nodded. "I see. Yes. A red Mazda."

"No," his Control said. "A black taxi."

There was a pause before Apple nodded again, once, on the word, "Ethel."

"I beg your pardon, Porter?"

Apple toadied by playing up to his chief's long-standing act of knowing nothing whatever about service slang, nick-names or gossip. He said:

"Ethel is a cab that was used in various clandestine operations for thirty years. She was being sold."

"So I have just been informed," Angus Watkin said. "And it appears that you, Porter, showed an inordinate interest in said vehicle, which in turn aroused the interest of the undercover gentlemen at the Yard."

"I understand now, sir."

"Therefore two men of the Special Branch were detailed to look into the curious matter."

Flaco and Gordo, Apple thought. Which explained their presence at the car auction and at Grinning Jim Jolly's sales lot. It also explained why they always seemed able to find their prey with such ease: their straight-in connection with the Metropolitan Police let them have every copper on the beat keeping a lookout for a red Mazda, number known. The only time he had been safe from being given away by the car was when it had been parked in a mews, or in Highgate, or in garages.

About to speak, Angus Watkin held off at a tap on the door. As if in punishment for the badly timed interruption, he let a pause grow before saying, "Enter."

The door opened. With the attitude of someone carrying at least a boar's head, Albert brought in a tray of tea-things. This he put down on a table at his chief's side and went silently out again.

Angus Watkin sat upright. Where another man might have rubbed his hands together, Watkin merely patted palm to palm like mordant clapping. He set about performing the tea ritual.

Beverage poured, he said while handing over cup and saucer, "You may smoke if you wish, Porter."

"I'm trying to give it up, sir," Apple said. "Thank you all the same." Apart from this being a good please-Watkin gambit, Apple felt that he had neither the energy nor the mental alertness to manage, all at the same time, a cigarette, the cup of tea, the need to blow smoke towards the fireplace, and the job of keeping up his end of the conversation. He would have preferred a nap.

Watkin sipped from his cup. He said, "I shall refrain from enquiring into your interest in the vehicle which has been retired from service."

"Thank you, sir."

"I shall simply mention that the procuring and collecting of artifacts which are related to past endeavours is frowned upon, though not forbidden."

Quietly, Apple said, "Yes, sir."

"Be that . . . as . . . it may," his Control said between sips of tea. "To return to the Special Branch. They did not know who you were. When word did finally get to the right ear and was returned, the Branch's two men were called off. Not too late, I trust?"

Apple shook his head, then nodded. He said, "Well, sir, as a matter of fact they did run quite a lot of interference. If it hadn't been for that . . ."

It was best left unfinished, Apple thought, the charge that for want of good liaison, which wasn't *his* fault, the mission might well have been brought to shining fruition. Every grotty little loophole helped.

"To be sure," Angus Watkin said—and the way he said it triggered a warning signal in Apple's mind.

Although Watkin had control at all times over his voice and his manner and his eyes and his features, individually, there were occasions when the undetectable in each joined the same in the others, thus creating a change strong enough to be noted—at least, to the educated and dedicated Watkin-watcher.

Being such himself, Apple became wary. He had the suspicion that something awful was on its way, and not the expected tongue-lashing for having failed as a kidnapper. This increased when Angus Watkin returned his cup and saucer to the tray instead of treating himself to a second pouring, as though he had treat enough already.

After gulping down the last of his tea, Apple said, "I think I will smoke after all, sir."

"By all means, Porter."

His crockery back on the tray, Apple got out his cigarettes and lit one. He drew deeply on the smoke, which he blew out in a long stream in the direction of the hearth, whose draught sucked it up the chimney. He attacked with:

"Yes, sir, it's too bad that the affair became complicated by this thing and that."

"It is indeed, Porter," Angus Watkin said. He leaned back in the chair. His heavy eyelids were sleepier than normal.

"But anyway," Apple offered with spread hands, "I'm sorry I didn't bring it off."

Watkin said, "I'm not."

"Er—what was that?"

His voice and mien, eyes and features joining to give away faintly that he was happy, Angus Watkin said, "I, Porter, am delighted that you failed."

Apple was so shocked he didn't realize how disrespectful was his position, how outraged his tone, how thoughtless his manner of smoking.

He had pulled himself forward to the edge of the seat, where he perched with head outthrust like a stalking wrestler's. His elbows on the chair arms, shoulders high, he took fast drags on his cigarette and let the exhaled smoke go where it would. He had already asked Angus Watkin sharply what he was talking about, getting no answer.

Now he said, "Do you mean to tell me that you didn't want me to bring off a kidnapping?" It was only by force of habit that he added, "Sir."

"I do mean to tell you that, Porter, yes," Angus Watkin said with false boredom.

"But—but—I nearly did."

"Really?"

"You know. The man that I . . . the man who played decoy." Watch it, he warned himself, beginning to calm.

"Ah yes, the man with the false moustache."

"I asked you for help and you gave it to me. That car and pair of operatives."

Watkin said suavely, "True, Porter, but the men I sent you were the worst I could find."

Apple gaped. He panned his gape around the room, took a final deep drag on his cigarette and threw it curtly into the fire. He asked, "They were?"

"The very worst, I assure you. It was their first time in the field. They were neophytes."

"But what if the decoy had been genuine, and the snatch had come off, or what if I'd managed to kidnap one of the Quartet later?" He wondered if he was making sense.

Mildly, Angus Watkin said, "If, Porter, you had by some chance brought me a victim of abduction, namely one of the Russian folk singers, I should have let him go."

Apple gaped again. "Eh?"

Watkin nodded. "And blamed his abduction on someone else, probably the Central Intelligence Agency."

Apple felt the return of his weariness and depression. He sank ponderously back in the chair. His hands he let dangle over the arms like bunches of asparagus.

He ought to have seen some of this before, Apple told himself. If a kidnap had been desired, Watkin would have pulled him out of the caper after the phony snatch attempt, it having presumedly made him known to the KGB.

Angus Watkin asked, "You see?"

Tiredly: "No, sir."

"Of course not. Therefore let me begin at the beginning, as the tale-spinners say." Putting his fingertips together, as though about to offer prayers that were full of holes, he went on easily:

"The four men who make up the Russian Rural Quartet were celebrated at the age of twenty-five, having been singing together for some years. But by the time they were thirty they were both famous and national heroes. They had added to their musical glory by having taken an active and prominent part in the Revolution. They became, and remain, members of the Communist Party.

"Even in Russia it is possible to marry well, and the singers did just that. Their connections were impeccable. They sired children who got the best available education, the finest opportunities, the most coveted posts and positions. These children themselves made marriages which, if such a thing is feasible, were even better.

"The offspring of these marriages couldn't go wrong. They were like princes of the realm, their credentials were so good. They rose at speed, and all of them became party members. These, the grandchildren of our folk singers, are now in their thirties and forties. Is all this clear so far, Porter?"

Apple scraped his stubble of hair on the chair back in nodding. Clear the narration was, but not to any point that he could fathom. Not that he cared particularly.

"It often happens," Angus Watkin said, "that grandparents and grandchildren are closer than parent and child, especially in regard to confidences and so forth. This obtains particularly in the Soviet Union, where family ties are unusually strong to begin with, and where senior members are treated with greater respect than in many other countries. It has proved useful."

Angus Watkin nodded. "But I must digress here a little to tell of the entry into the tale of a British Intelligence operative."

"Me, sir?"

"No, Porter, not you. He is a high-grade agent who has lived in Moscow for many years."

Apple said a lifeless, "Oh."

"We'll call the operative Gerald," Watkin went on. "Over a period of time, one by one, he got to know the Russian Rural Quartet. Slowly he cultivated their friendship and gained their confidence. He admitted to them at last—a lie, as we know—that he was in the KGB, and a high-ranking officer, at that.

"Gerald told the four old men that they could give invaluable help to Mother Russia, if they were so inclined. Spies, subversives and plain malingerers were to be found at all levels, he said, but particularly on the upper levels inhabited by the singers' grandchildren—in the military, heavy industry, science and in medicine. Still clear?"

"Yes, sir."

"All that the four men need do, Gerald told them, was to take careful note of the news and gossip that was retailed to them by their children's issue, which retailing was constant and fulsome, the relationships being close. Gerald made it clear, naturally, that no one must know how he and the four were involved, that even his own underlings didn't know. None of the grandchildren, fortunately, are connected with the KGB."

Dully, Apple supposed that Josef's easy agreement to the meeting in Muswell Hill must have been because he accepted the tall stranger as a connection of Gerald's. So even that had been no accomplishment.

Apple sighed.

Angus Watkin asked, "I'm not boring you, am I, Porter?"

"No, sir. Not at all. Please continue."

"Thank you. But where was I exactly?"

A test. Apple passed it with, "The grandchildren having no doings with the KGB."

"Quite so," his Control said. "Now. A great deal of sensitive information was coming to Gerald through the singers. In time, he realized that he would have to find out if the men were genuinely anti-West. If, in fact, they were passing on straight data rather than merely giving him what they thought he wanted to hear.

"Therefore it occurred to me that the best way to show how they stood was to tempt them with the chance of living on this side of the Iron Curtain. Does that strike you as reasonable, Porter?"

"Yes, sir."

Watkin said blandly, flatly, "So I sent you in with orders to perform a kidnapping."

Apple shook his head. "I'm lost."

"It's quite simple, Porter. I am, you see, familiar with your character. I was aware that, because of the type of person you are, you would not be able to bring yourself to abduct one of the old men."

Apple said another bloodless, "Oh."

"You would, I knew, try persuasion. You would try to sell defection to the singers. And you would do it earnestly, even desperately, seeing it as the only solution to the mission—as far as you yourself were concerned. Whereas any other operative I might have used would have offered defection with a smoothness that could have been seen through by those shrewd old men. You were the best choice because of, shall we say, your penchant for sentimentality."

Apple gave several slow and dreary blinks. He felt that he couldn't be put down any lower. He felt used and abused. He felt peeled and sliced and shredded.

"Your attempt failed, happily," Angus Watkin said. "The Russian Rural Quartet will be a valuable source of information for as long as they live."

A silence fell. As it grew, Apple realized that he was expected to make some sort of comment, perhaps in a congratulatory vein. He roused himself, sat up loosely, thought about it. Nothing came, except:

"And that's what the mission was all about?"

"Quite so."

"And now it's over?"

"Over and done. Mission accomplished."

Yours at any rate, Apple thought. He asked, "Is there anything else, sir?"

"Nothing, Porter. I have told you all there is."

Apple pushed himself heavily up to his feet. "Then if you'll excuse me."

"Of course," Angus Watkin said, tapping his fingertips together. "Have a pleasant supper."

Mumbling: "Thank you."

"Also, Porter, please give my regards to your dog."

Still mumbling: "I shall."

"I do not, I confess, know the animal's name," Watkin said. "What is it, Porter?"

Apple felt as if his shredded self had been put through a blender, from which the final drops of liquid were being implacably shaken. He was too spent to experience surprise on hearing himself answer the question at once, with, "Monico."

The sole defence that Apple could fumblingly muster was that this was where Angus Watkin showed why he had climbed to the attic Upstairs.

"Monico," Watkin repeated in a way that suggested he would never forget the name. "Thank you, Porter."

"Welcome."

"And good night."

"Good night, sir," Apple whispered, going to the door. He left the room without looking back at his chief, whom he hated even while admitting that the man did have a mysterious power, which was better for Apple than seeing himself as having a mundane weakness.

As Apple closed the door behind him, Albert appeared from another room. The older man glanced up with a smile on lips that were poised for a quip. The glance became a look, the smile died, the quip went undelivered. He turned and moved towards the front door.

Apple followed. Afraid of hate, he was busy trying to force Angus Watkin out of the fore of his mind. It wasn't easy. His mind was too full of darkness for him to see which way to do the forcing.

Albert had the door open.

Apple reminded himself that not everything in his present world was dark and grim. After all, he did have a supper engagement with a woman who was not only attractive, but gifted and compassionate as well.

Feeling less of a damp nothing, Apple exchanged nods with Albert as he went by. Through the door-frame he stopped. He stood on the outside step and breathed deeply of the cool night air. At the same time, he squared his shoulders. That was for show. He sagged again when he heard the door click shut.

So get moving, he told himself. No sense in hanging around this place.

In patting his pockets to find the keys to the Mazda, Apple caused a crinkle sound. He recalled the envelope that he had picked up at Harlequin Mansions. Bringing it out idly, thumbing open the flap, he extracted a piece of paper and peered at it in the dim light.

From the office of Grinning Jim Jolly, the letter informed Appleton Porter, Esq., that his offer for the ex-taxi had been accepted.

Apple smiled. After a second reading of the letter, plus a thought of thanks sent to the car-lot secretary, he carefully and fondly replaced the paper in its envelope, which he returned to his pocket.

Apple took a deeper breath of night air, gave his shoulders a true squaring and made to go forward.

And froze.

He was not alone.

Beside the first of the miniature trees on his right, a figure was standing. In the dimness it was discernible merely as a human shape, probably male.

Apple cleared his throat. It sounded like the complaint of a sleeper who was being disturbed. What kept Apple from strong worry was the thought that the safe-house possibly always had an outside guard.

That lasted for seven seconds, up until Apple noticing the other figure.

No clearer than the first, it stood on the opposite side of the path that led to the gate, also beside a tree, also with a maleness.

A pair of guards was unlikely, Apple mused, unless they were split, one usually at the front and one at the rear. He said a tentative, "Well . . ."

The first figure moved. It swayed backwards and forwards, as though that were needed as a prelude to speech, which came next. The voice was male, the language Russian.

"Good evening, Jim," the man said.

Apple's worry eased and he made to answer the greeting. Before he could, the other figure spoke up, in the same language and also with a male deepness:

"Yes, Jim, good evening."

Again Apple started to reply, answer both greetings, and again was forestalled, this time by another voice. It came from a third, unseen man who was somewhere near the gate. He said, in Russian:

"Let's get on with it, lads."

Apple slowly shook his head. "This can't be true," he said in the same language.

The first man said, "It is."

Apple: "Come into the light, please. All of you."

By two of them taking a step out from the trees, by the other coming forward from the gate, the three men showed themselves. They were Josef's folk-singing colleagues.

"You're right," Apple said. "It's true."

"Yes, Jim, here we are."

"But how?"

The trio took turns:

"We followed you in a taxi from the hotel where we had that banquet."

"When the driver lost you we started looking on foot. In the end we found your red car."

"We've been waiting here for you to come out."

Apple took another deep breath. It was for calm. His excitement was growing. He held back the question he wanted to ask, out of dread that he might be wrong, but made a mute request by spreading his arms.

Beginning, as before, with the first, nearest old man, the trio said:

"We saw you for the first time at Peace Manor, that place we were staying at."

"You were watching through the greenhouse window."

"We thought you were KGB."

Apple dropped his arms. "I'm not."

"We know that now, Jim."

"We knew it soon after that."

"Josef told us."

Carefully, Apple asked, "What, exactly, did Josef tell you about me, gentlemen?"

The first folk singer said, "That you'd offered to help him."

The second folk singer said, "In case he wanted to stay in the West."

The third folk singer said, "Defect, lads, is the word."

Still with care, but with his hope and excitement hopping, Apple said, "Call it anything you like. A change in life-style is pleasant. And yes, Josef was right. I do help people who want to move."

In a unison that was as imperfect as their singing, the trio said, "Good."

Apple plunged and asked the question. "Do you want to stay out of Russia?"

"We didn't until we heard about this help."

"We've had many long talks about it."

"We want to defect."

Apple let his feelings flow and his smile blossom. "Well now, that is nice."

The three men said:

"We've been trying to get to talk to you for days."

"You kept avoiding us."

"Suspicious, you were."

Earnestly, Apple said, "No, gentlemen, simply cautious. One is unable to accept easily that people dislike their own countries."

The trio said:

"Oh no, we don't dislike Russia."

"We think it's a wonderful country."

"We think it's the greatest country in the world and has the finest political system."

Apple asked, "But you want something else?"

The first old man said, "We want to spend our declining years somewhere warm. Romantic. Exotic."

The second old man said, "Palm trees, white sand, soft music and grass skirts."

The third old man said, "Bare tits."

Apple nodded. "All that is understandable, gentlemen. And possible, though I can't make promises."

"That doesn't matter."

"You'll do your best, we know."

"See, Jim, we trust you."

Apple felt the faint pricklings of a blush. He coughed and said, "Well, thank you. Most kind. But how can you trust me when you haven't talked to me until now?"

The trio said:

"It's as plain as day in your gaze, Jim."

"It's there in your eyes for the astute to see."

"Yes, you have good eyes."

Apple nodded shrewdly. What they meant, he mused, was that his eyes showed that he was a man of determination and drive, a man who could be trusted to make the right, professional moves, a man with whom the timid and uncertain would be safe.

Apple, joyful, bowed. "Welcome to the West, gentlemen," he said. "My chief *will* be pleased to see you."

In ragged unison: "Thank you very much."

As Apple, turning, pressed hard on the doorbell, he recognized the joy in him as a negative. The feeling was, in fact, a malicious and vengeful glee.

Apple blinked slowly, hurt.

ABOUT THE AUTHOR

Marc Lovell is the author of four previous Appleton Porter novels, *Apple Spy in the Sky, Spy on the Run, The Spy with His Head in the Clouds,* and *The Spy Game,* as well as many others, including *Hand over Mind* and *A Voice from the Living*. Mr. Lovell has lived on the island of Majorca for the last twenty years.